THE LEGENDS OF REGIA
FOREST FIRE

a novel
TENAYA JAYNE

COLD FIRE PUBLISHING LLC

Other titles by Tenaya Jayne

Blue Aspen
The Slayer's Wife
Forbidden Forest

COLD FIRE PUBLISHING, LLC

ISBN: 978-0-9882757-3-7

Edited by Finish The Story
Proofread by TK
Cover art by Wicked Cover Designs

For Stephanie- a princess in her own right.

Prologue

"Protect the prince!"

Redge's yelling voice was the best sound Syrus had ever heard. Fighting erupted around them but rather than join in, Syrus pulled Forest tighter into his chest. He was whole now. He was hers, and she would always possess him. Chaos, danger, and death reigned all around, yet there was nothing but silence and peace inside him.

Redge opened the End of the Bridge.

The harsh wind pulled them into the portal, but with Forest in Syrus' arms, he felt shielded from it. They were encapsulated in the heart of the raging noise. Regrettably, his vision would fade soon. He wanted to use the time to get lost in Forest's eyes, but she had her face buried in his chest, so he contented himself with watching her hair dance in the wind around them.

The soldiers in the portal tumbled in disarray. Mesmerized by Forest, Syrus didn't react fast enough to stop the foot of one from slamming into the back of her head. He felt the force of the blow in his own head, coupled with an insane fury that she had been hurt. She had been clinging tightly to him but now her arms were limp.

He didn't fear for her life. Since they had forged their connections, he would know if her life was in danger and the extent of any injury she might suffer without ever having to see it; the knowledge was innate. His heart could feel the beating of hers. The blow to her head had only knocked her unconscious.

In the next second, the portal dumped them and the whole troop of soldiers in a heap in the throne room of the Onyx Castle. Syrus' sight blurred around the edges. The soldiers untangled themselves and rose to their feet, leaving Syrus in the middle of the floor, cradling Forest against him. He tipped her head back and gazed at her face for the last remaining moments of his vision. He was only dimly aware of the movement and talk around him. The unmistakable lilt of his mother's voice was trying to break its way into his attention. He paid no mind. The world was nothing, there was only Forest. He stroked her cheek with the pads of his fingers and kissed her lips.

"I demand to know what is going on!" Christiana yelled. "Syrus! Syrus, stop it! You debase yourself in public! Get off the floor! Let go of that disgusting aberration! Syrus!"

The only thing his mother said that registered in his brain was the insult to Forest.

"She's my destined life mate, mother," he said calmly, without taking his eyes from Forest.

"No!" she screamed in a whisper. "No! It can't be!" She turned her wide furious eyes on Redge.

Redge merely shrugged.

"Syrus, it's not the truth," she said with forced composure. "You've been bewitched. You're sick, and you need medical attention."

Christiana clapped her hands, and five ogres came rushing forward. Syrus looked up and saw Redge fleeing the throne room.

Christiana sent the soldiers away before giving the ogres any orders. The less witnesses the better. She pointed at Syrus. "All right. Three of you take the prince to his chambers and keep him there. Subdue him if necessary, but do not let him out."

Syrus' vision darkened down to blurs and shadows. Everything he'd just gone through left him too weak to have a prayer of fighting off three ogres. Six huge hands grabbed him. "NO! NO! Mother, don't do this!" His heart cried out as loud as his lungs as Forest was wrenched from his arms. "FOREST! FOREST!"

The last thing Syrus saw was Forest lying unconscious on the floor with his mother standing triumphantly over her. Then his eyes slid into darkness. His cries reverberated through the whole castle until he was shut in and locked down.

****

Forest's eyelids fluttered and she moaned. Christiana grabbed her roughly by the shoulders, lifted her, then slammed her head back down on the floor, knocking her unconscious again.

"Now, one of you, get this piece of filth out of my throne room," Christiana ordered.

"What shall we do with her?"

"Christiana!" Zeren barged into the room with Redge on his heels. "What is going on here?" Zeren looked down at Forest and then over to the ogres waiting to do the queen's bidding. "Put her in a clean room and get her a doctor. No harm is to come to her. "

The ogres looked uncertainly at the queen.

"Now!" Zeren yelled.

Forest was picked up and taken from the room.

"Now." Zeren turned his attention on his wife. "Tell me what is going on. Where's Syrus?"

"He was injured. He is resting in his chambers," she said innocently.

"Remember your place, Christiana," Zeren said sternly. "I'm going to see my son." He turned to leave the room as a messenger came rushing in.

"Your highness! Fighting has broken out in the shifter colonies. Philippe's armies are moving out. They march on Kyhael!"

Zeren looked momentarily torn before turning to Redge. "Come with me."

The two men left the room without a backward glance at the queen.

"Give me orders, my king," Redge said.

"I want you to stay close to Syrus. Pay attention to what the queen does. I don't want her interfering in anything."

"Yes, my king."

Zeren grabbed Redge firmly by the shoulder. "Do everything you can to keep things neutral here, everything in your power. Christiana has no authority to relieve you of your position. Don't let her harm the young woman that came back with Syrus."

Redge nodded and Zeren rushed off to confer with his generals.

Chapter One

The Werewolf Lair

The aquamarine moonlight reached down, caressing Netriet as she lay on the stone floor. She ached to open the closed balcony doors and let the moonlight fill the room, but the chain around her wrist would not permit it. She was beyond the pain. The cold of the stone under her clawed deep into the tissue of her flesh for hours and hours, finally releasing her to the pleasure of numbness. Perhaps this would be her last night. She turned aside her feelings of failure and let her eyes slide out of focus in the beautifully dim light.

She was positive she had missed her window to kill Philippe. He'd left two days ago in a towering rage after learning Forest had lied, escaped his grasp, and he'd lost the collar in the process. She'd heard the movement of the army far below her at the base of the mountain, but now all was quiet. Death moved around the edges of the room, whispering peaceful seductions. Her eyelids became heavier and heavier with every blink. Sleep descended as gently as the moonlight.

"Nettie," his voice sounded strained. "Nettie, wake up."

The smell of blood woke her more efficiently than his shaking her. Philippe's face was close to hers when she opened her eyes, his beard tickling her neck. He had come back. Either that or she was dreaming. He stank of blood and sweat. A dirty gash stretched across his forehead, and fingernail scratches extended down his cheeks.

"So," she said weakly as he picked her up off the floor. "You didn't forget me after all."

"No, I was…"

Netriet reached up and gently caressed his face. His eyebrows pulled down as his black eyes bore sharply into hers. He searched her face for a moment before a small smile pulled into one side of his mouth.

"I have wondered," he said quietly. "I thought it might be like that." He hoisted her up and crushed her mouth in a harsh kiss.

Netriet felt smothered under his ardor as he dumped her on the bed. "Wait," she said desperately as he pulled his cloak from his shoulders and dropped it to the floor.

"What?"

She held up her wrist. "Please take it off."

He narrowed his eyes for a second then shrugged and went to get the key from across the room. Her arm was freed, and he again smothered her. She let her muscles go lax, and she lay there like a corpse.

He noticed soon enough. "What's wrong with you?" he demanded.

"I'm just so weak. I haven't eaten in days and days. I'm sorry. I *really* want to participate."

He smiled broadly and pulled his shirt over his head. His torso was covered in deep purple bruises.

"What happened to you?" she asked.

"Here." He offered her his forearm.

She sat up a little and sank her teeth deep into his flesh. This was the opportunity she had been waiting for. She pulled as hard as she could on his veins.

"My position was challenged," he explained. "I had to fight two contenders. They're both dead now. The army is marching to Kyhael. I will join them tomorrow, but I had to come back to tie up a few loose ends. I've got to get the...the...uh..."

It was starting to work. Netriet pulled harder and harder. She had never taken this much blood at one time from anyone. She looked up at his face. His eyes turned glassy. She continued to drain him.

"Those idiots keep using the wrong words. I swear it didn't take me half this time to become…become fluent in French. I don't think they…um…understand why I made them…I mean…aren't you done yet?"

He was on the brink. She felt flooded, but with two more deep pulls, he would be right where she wanted him. He stroked the back of her head and then staggered to the side, pulling his arm from her mouth. She sat upright, her strength returned, but she felt nauseated. He looked at her confusedly, his eyes dilated.

"Come here. Lie down. You need to rest," she said.

He obeyed her instantly. "Yes. I'm so tired."

Philippe lay down next to her. All his carnal intentions had vanished, and he closed his eyes. She smiled to herself. He'd been so arrogant before, insisting that if she bit him, she'd have no persuasion over him. What a crock. She sat still for a moment. There were numbers of things she could do to kill him, but she wanted to make sure that when he was found, his death would be one of humiliating circumstances. A new werewolf leader would emerge, but with Philippe dead, there would be discord. The new leader would need time to establish his authority and make changes to the whole community. The future of Regia lay in her hands, well, her hand.

She watched his chest rise and fall and considered the matter carefully. The vampires would write songs in her honor. Oh, that would just burn the queen's ass. No one even knew she was still alive and she was about to hand her race the war.

For the next hour, Netriet monitored Philippe's vital signs. She continued to take blood from him to keep him right on that dangerous edge. Everything still seemed quiet and empty in the mountain, but she locked the heavy doors and slid a long sword through the handles just in case. She kept the setup simple. She unhooked the chain that had held her captive all this time from the wall and dragged it out onto the balcony. It would be an adequate trip line.

Netriet gazed into the night sky and out over the land. She could see Halussis like a speck in the distance. *Home*, she thought. *Goodbye*.

She positioned herself at the very edge of the balcony. The updraft of the wind gusting against the rock face of the mountain threatened to pull her over the side. Bracing her hand on the cut stone railing, She began whispering. "Philippe," she urged her voice into his dreams. "Wake up, Philippe."

He sat up and looked for her in the darkness.

"Come to me, Philippe. Come…"

Philippe stood up; his body propelled haphazardly toward her.

"Hurry!" she ordered.

She braced herself as his bulk moved hurriedly to her. Would the chain hold? She held her breath. His foot caught. He tripped, slamming into her. His arms flailing, Philippe grabbed her, and clasped her tightly against his chest as they went over the edge. Tangled together, Netriet and Philippe fell to their deaths.

****

Awareness was hateful. The unconscious filling of her lungs pulled life into Netriet's broken body, unwilling to let her die. She opened her swollen eyes. Oh, she knew this was no dream. The pain was indescribable. She lifted her head a fraction. Philippe lay smashed sickeningly beneath her. His black hole eyes pointed to the sky, lifeless. She lifted her arm and closed his eyelids with her fractured hand, the misplaced bones grinding together.

She had a choice. She could lay and wait for someone to come along and kill her or she could attempt to escape.

Netriet moved slowly, surveying the damage through her body: seven broken fingers, a few broken ribs, probable internal bleeding, and one broken foot. She didn't count being covered in bruises and lacerations. It was pointless. The sensible thing to do was remain still and pray death circled back around quickly and finished what it started.

The sun began coloring the sky in morning. Holding her screams inside her throat, she forced herself to stand. The damage was more severe than she had originally thought. The ground undulated under her feet. Blood rose up her throat and filled her mouth. She limped toward the Wolf's Wood. Her insides smashed to paste. She would not last the day, but if she could die inside the boundary of the Wood, her soul would be happy there.

Delirium overtook her, but she continued to limp along, leaving a trail of blood behind. The sweet foliage cushioned her as she lay on the ground. *Such beauty*, she thought. *I'm happy to die here.* A gentle breeze swirled around her and began to whisper.

A large pair of eyes swam in Netriet's vision, insect-like and transparent.

"Hello, Netriet."

"Am I dead?"

"Very nearly, but I won't let you."

Netriet's eyes rolled back, as she lapsed into unconsciousness. Shi, the dryad ghost, guardian of the Wolf's Wood, sighed and began putting the young woman back together.

****

"Syrus..." Forest whispered. "Kiss me."

He could see her clearly in the dark, her long tresses falling over her shoulders, her eyes spreading madness in his mind, beckoning him. But every time he reached for her, his fingers drifted through her and she vanished.

Loneliness had crystallized inside Syrus' blood. The spiked edges lacerated him with every beat of his heart. But the dark womb offered no warmth or comfort. His mind was stuck on an infinite loop that caused terrible agony and sorrow. *Forest.* His self-induced hallucinations of her were a double-edged sword that cut going in and coming out, but he couldn't find the power to stop them. Physically, he was weak like an old man. The cell made his mage power useless. He could do nothing but wait.

Chapter Two

Austin, TX

The Austin mall was a well-oiled machine. All the gears were moving in the usual half-asleep speed of its morning workers. A handful of elderly mall walkers in jogging suits shuffled along the paths outside the locked gates of the stores, having conversations about their lap dogs and grandchildren. Music blasted from store to store on the second level, a rotten garble of conflicting songs as the employees waged war against each other with the sound waves.

Mindy Stern was running late. She parked her beat-up mid-nineties Civic at the far end of the lot so her car would be in the shade. The shade would be worth the hike by the afternoon, but as it was summer, it didn't matter that it was still only eight-thirty in the morning; she was sweating by the time she reached the entrance. It would have made more sense for her to be wearing a sundress with sandals, but that was the opposite kind of look her job required.

A Styrofoam cup of coffee in each hand prevented her from opening the doors. She thrust her combat boot against the button that opened the doors for wheelchairs and was blasted with a welcoming gust of air conditioning. She passed two elderly women and muttered, "Good morning."

Neither responded with words but raised their penciled eyebrows as they surveyed her appearance and lifted their noses in the air. Mindy rolled her eyes as the sound of the women's windbreakers swished away. She imagined the snotty old bitties taking a wrong turn into her shop and falling over dead with shock and outrage.

She climbed the escalator, which hadn't been turned on yet, and strolled down to Hot Topic. She had only been the assistant manager for a month, but she found the small amount of power agreeable on most days. Rachel was already in the store, and Mindy was keen to question her, since the last Vampire RPG they had hosted together had ended *strangely*. Mindy had tried to reach Rachel through calls, texts, emails, and Facebook, but Rachel had fallen off the radar for the whole weekend.

Mindy set her coffee cups down, opened the gate halfway, grabbed her coffees, and kicked the gate back down behind her. She instantly hesitated at the soft uneven sounds of crying coming from the back of the store. She sighed, realizing the day would be filled with drama as she walked through the store and turned into the back room.

Rachel sat on the floor, her checkered stocking-clad legs stretched straight out in front of her. Mindy blinked, instantly alarmed at her friend's appearance. Her heavy eyeliner ran down her cheeks and her thick black hair hung in a greasy mess. She was wearing the same purple lace corset and banana yellow skirt that Mindy had last seen her in. Worse than the fact that she'd obviously not changed her clothes or bathed in three days, she looked sick: pale, waxy, and anemic. Her hands shook as she sorted through a box of small miscellaneous clearance items.

"Rachel?"

"Pandora!" Rachel sobbed.

"Huh?"

"I'm legally changing my name to Pandora. I told you that."

"Oh, right. Sorry. I forgot."

Rachel dropped a marked-down jar of Edward body glimmer to the floor and put both hands over her face, her shoulders shaking with tears.

Mindy sat down beside her and patted her knee. "What's wrong?"

Rachel picked the jar back up and thrust it in Mindy's face. "That's what I wanted."

Mindy raised one eyebrow. "Then buy it. It's only a dollar."

"No, I wanted *that*." She pointed to the label, her finger tapping Rob Pattinson's face.

Mindy's raised eyebrow shot up a bit further. "Yeah, well, get in line."

"No, no. You don't understand," Rachel wailed. "I finally meet a real vampire but does he want to fall in love with me? No! Is he tortured by abstaining from my alluring smell? No! Does he want to steal me away from everyone and everything and protect me? No! No! No! I wanted Edward, or Stefan, or Eric Northman, and what did I get? Dracula, that's what! Old black and white horror movie Dracula!"

"Uh, Rachel, have you been experimenting with drugs?"

"Drugs? No. Why?"

"Well, first of all, you look like hell. Second, you obviously haven't bathed in a while. And third, *real* vampires?"

"Look!" Rachel pulled up her sleeve. Her arm was covered in bruised bite marks.

"Holy shit!"

"And here." She moved her hair aside and pulled down her collar, exposing the top of her shoulder.

Mindy took a deep breath. "Okay, Rachel, have you thought about calling the cops? Why would you let some sicko do this to you?"

"I didn't let him!"

"Really?"

"Okay, I let him the first time cause he was so hot, but then it was like I had no choice. He tells me what to do, and I flippin' do it! I can't seem to disobey him." She erupted into tears again, covering her face with her hands.

"Is he staying at your apartment?" Mindy asked.

"Yeah."

Mindy pulled out her phone. "Okay, well, I'm going to call the cops and have them go over to your place."

Rachel quickly grabbed her hand, crushing Mindy's finger's painfully around the phone. "No, you can't!"

"Why not?"

"He'll kill them all! He told me he would kill anyone who tried to take him away from me."

"Yeah, all the more reason to call the cops. He's threatening you and others. He's a psycho!"

"No, you don't get it, Mindy. Leith's not a psycho, he's a *real* vampire."

Mindy sat back and rolled her gum around in her mouth. She looked at Rachel's arm again and winced. Her friend was in serious trouble, whether she was telling the truth or not. She knew Rachel *believed* she was telling the truth, and obviously, Rachel hadn't been biting herself. Someone was preying on her, and he had to be stopped.

"Okay, let's suspend reality for a second here and say I believe you. The bottom line is there is a man assaulting you and squatting in your apartment. Who may or may not be a killer. We have to find a way to get rid of him. Do you want me to call Danny and have him go over and rough this guy up?"

"No! Danny's big, but Leith would smash him. I'm sure of it. I don't want Danny getting hurt." Rachel pulled her knees up and rested her head against them, sobbing quietly.

Mindy looked at her watch and huffed in exasperation. She had to open the store. And she had to help her friend. Rachel was in no shape to work, but Mindy couldn't send her home while there was a whack job with overdeveloped jaw muscles there.

"Look, I have to open the store now. I don't want you on the floor today. Just stay back here and do inventory," Mindy said.

Rachel nodded and turned her attention back to the box of clearance items.

"I don't want you going anywhere. Okay?"

"Huh?"

"I'm going to help you, somehow, but I need to know that I can trust you not to sneak off and go back home."

Rachel sighed listlessly and twisted a strand of greasy hair around her finger. "I promise."

Shoppers were light through the store that morning, and the quiet time allowed Mindy to do some web searching for possible ways to eradicate a "vampire." She also had to ask Rachel questions frequently about her vamp's habits and weaknesses. Mindy was surprised that the nut ball claimed the sun would kill him. Nowadays, the sun issue was so old school. She became frustrated very quickly as 99.9% of what she found was about online gaming or RPGs. Finally, she gave her iPhone to Rachel and told her to sift through the mire on the web. The store manager, Scott, had agreed to come in and cover for her at lunch so she could try to sort out Rachel's problem.

In the food court, Mindy plunked a huge double bacon burger in front of Rachel, while she stuck to sucking down a diet soda. Rachel was still surfing the web on Mindy's phone.

"Have you found anything?" Mindy asked.

"Maybe. See what you think." Rachel handed the phone back and dubiously eyed the burger on the table for a second. Mindy was about to point out how feeble and anemic Rachel looked but before she could say anything, Rachel picked it up and tried to swallow the half-pound mound of meat whole.

Mindy looked down at her phone and what Rachel had found. She snorted loudly. "Craigslist? Really, Rachel?"

"Just read it," Rachel said through her mouth of food. "And it's Pandora."

"Yeah, yeah," Mindy said absently, reading the classified listing.

Real vampires hooked their teeth in you? Experienced, legitimate vampire slayer. Have weapons, will travel. Reasonable rates. Free phone consultation. Call Forest. (812) 555-9344

Mindy looked up at Rachel.

"Maybe it's bogus. But we could call and see what we thought then." Rachel said.

"We're not calling from my phone!" Mindy said severely. "I don't want this person having my phone number."

"So block the number. What's the big deal?"

"With my luck, they'd be able to crack right through that, and the next thing I know I've got a 'vampire slayer' stalking me. Where's your phone?"

"I don't know. I haven't been able to find it since Leith came home with me. I think I lost it. There's a payphone on the lower level."

"Okay, we'll call from there."

****

Forest slumped in a chair in the corner of her bedroom with her chin resting on her chest, her eyes half open. A loaded shotgun lay next to her feet atop a pile of shells and empty ammunition boxes. She'd been holding her nine millimeter for so long it felt fused to her hand. Various other weapons littered the floor around her: knives, a hunting bow and quiver, a mace, and even a replica of a Viking war hammer that she'd bought at a renaissance fair. It was lucky for her that vampire's bodies fell to ash a few hours after death; otherwise, she would have been hard pressed to dispose of all of the bodies in her condo. As it was, the recent purchase of a commercial sized Shop-Vac proved to be money well spent.

She stretched and yawned. The pain was worse today. The only thing Forest had found to take the edge off the agony of being so far away from Syrus was sleeping. But Queen Christiana's antics had made sleeping something of the past for Forest. Her whole chest felt like a huge open mouth. She had no way to feed it. No way to close it. No way to ignore it. *I can't take this anymore; I can't take this anymore.* Those words never seemed to stop repeating inside her head since she'd been banished from Regia… from Syrus. But she had no choice but to take it. Take it, and take it, and take it.

When Forest did sleep, her dreams were filled with Syrus, and for those fleeting moments in her subconscious there was peace and passion laced with a sweet aching. In her dreams, they were together back at her cottage. She'd see flashes of his smiles, hear his voice, feel his lips on her neck where no scars stood between them. Being enveloped in his arms, resting her head against his chest with his heartbeat pounding next to her ear, and then waking up alone, more alone than she'd ever been in her life was an unspeakable torture. Opening your eyes after sleeping, your heart choking and tears soaking your pillow was even less of an incentive to sleep than being caught off-guard by one of Christiana's assassins.

Forest had been forced to kill at least two assassins a day, sometimes more since she'd been shoved back here. Oddly enough, she didn't find pleasure in killing vampires anymore. Mating with Syrus had caused her to change sides. Vampires were her people now. There was only one she wanted to kill: Leith. Forest didn't really even want Christiana dead; she just wanted her to stop. She imagined her hands around Christiana's little neck more than a few times, but in reality, even if she had the chance, Forest's love for Syrus would stop her from killing his mother.

Forest knew something had happened to Syrus. She knew he was alive, she could feel it, but he hadn't broken through her banishment yet. Someone or something had tied his hands. He was surrounded by darkness that had nothing to do with his blindness. Redge told her that even he couldn't find Syrus, but he knew he was in the castle, somewhere.

She had to do something to take back control of her life, but she had no idea how. Banishment effectively ended her job with Fortress. She didn't need to worry about money, but she feared her sanity was starting to jitter like a Chihuahua, seeing as she had nothing to do except wait for the next sucker to fall through her ceiling. She got out occasionally, but when she left, the assassins began to add up, and it was a chore to hack through them all. Moving might have been the logical thing to do, but she was afraid if she left, Syrus wouldn't be able to find her.

She sighed and rubbed her scars, the urge to tear at her skin pulsing through her fingernails. Hatred was too weak a word for what she felt towards the ridges disfiguring her neck and shoulder. Maybe one day, in some distant impossible future, the ties that bound her to Leith would be broken.

Her phone vibrated in her pocket, and she quickly snatched it out, hoping it was Redge or Kendel, her previous Regian manager, with some good news. Her caller ID didn't recognize the caller. "Hello?"

"Um. Hi. I was calling about the ad in Craigslist."

"Oh. Yeah. Okay."

"Can I talk to Forest?"

"This is Forest."

"Oh. Okay, well I just wanted to know if it's a joke."

Forest sighed. This wasn't the first call she'd gotten like this since she put that ad up. It had been Kendel's idea that she freelance. "No. It's not a joke. Do you have a vampire problem?"

"Yeah, well, my friend does. She's covered in bite marks."

"Can I talk to her?" Forest asked. "Is she there?"

There was some scuffling noise as the phone was passed over.

"Hello?"

Forest reminded herself she was talking to humans. If she was polite, they would just about tell her anything. "Hi there. I'm Forest. What's your name?"

"Uh, Pandora." She said it like a question.

"Tell me about your vampire problem."

"I met him a few days ago, and now he's in my apartment, and he won't leave. I was kinda open to the idea of being with a vampire. I let him bite me, but he's so violent, and he orders me around. I can't stop myself—I do what he tells me." The girl sounded shaky. "Do you really think you can get rid of him for me?"

"Sure. I used to do it professionally."

Forest could almost hear the look of incredulity fall on the girl's face.

"Hold on a sec."

The girl's friend was asking questions in the background.

"Um, the ad said reasonable rates. What does that mean? Could you give me a ballpark figure?"

Before Forest could answer, she heard the other girl in the background suggest they forget this and just call the cops.

"I told you, Leith warned me about calling the cops. I don't think you—"

"Hey!" Forest half yelled into the phone.

"Yeah?"

"Your vampire's name is Leith?"

"Yeah, at least that's what he said it was. Why?"

"I'll do the job for free," Forest said quickly. "Just give me the address. He'll be gone within the hour."

"Um, okay. Why?"

"Let's just say I've got a slight grudge against him."

Chapter Three

Kyhael, Regia

Zefyre twisted the pages of her report into a tight scroll as she walked into the *Rune-dy's* main meeting room, knowing it may be the last time she set foot there. She couldn't imagine any way this meeting could result in anything good for her. She'd taken the fact that her brother, Rahaxeris, was the high priest for granted and given herself too great a license. Icy fear sluiced down her back as her eyes fell on her brother sitting stone still across the room. Zefyre squared her shoulders, forcing herself forward to hand him her report.

Rahaxeris' face remained impassive as he read Zefyre's report, but his hands shook infinitesimally on the edge of the parchment. This almost imperceptible loss of control sent a sharp wave of terror through Zefyre. She had to fight the urge to stammer out apologies and excuses.

"Tell me, Zefyre, are you laboring under your own vision of the future?"

"No, sir."

He looked at her over the edge of the paper. "You never reported to me that you were sending Philippe sacrificial messengers."

"Well...I..."

Rahaxeris lifted his index finger to silence her and looked back down at the parchment. "I see what you were doing, and I might have sanctioned it, but you went around me. And you obviously chose poorly whom you sent to him."

"Yes, sir. Netriet was a mistake. I never anticipated Philippe would keep her alive, let alone form some aberrant attachment to her."

"A mistake *I* would not have made."

"Yes, sir."

"And now look at the high price of your mistake. Philippe is dead and confusion is rampant through the ranks of the werewolves. Dissention and argument over who is the new pack leader, and while they scrabble, Zeren is stomping them into the ground."

Zefyre shuffled her feet and looked at the floor.

"Have you located Netriet yet?"

"No, sir."

Rahaxeris sighed irritably. "You've left me no other alternative than to work with Zeren." The parchment in his hands erupted into flames. He held it until it burned down to nothing. "This altering of plans displeases me, Zefyre." He took another long breath. "Now, tell me of my daughter and her mate."

"They both suffer with severe separation sickness. Christiana has imprisoned Syrus inside a portal that goes nowhere. No one can reach him. She sent Redge to the front lines. And while Syrus is caged, and Zeren is away, she is opening special portals and giving vampires the freedom to circumvent traffic controllers. She dumps assassins daily, directly into Forest's dwelling on Earth."

"And so far Forest has come through unharmed?" he asked.

"Yes, sir."

An undeniable look of pride came onto Rahaxeris' face. "Are you in touch with her?"

"No, sir. She won't talk to me. She doesn't trust me. She communicates only with Kendel. Shall I break Christiana's banishment and bring her back?"

"No. We need to break Syrus out first. We'll let him bring her back."

"Forgive me, sir, but how are you going to break Syrus out? Christiana will admit no one into the Onyx Castle."

Rahaxeris gave her a withering look. "Do you think I can't get past that feeble, usurping hag? I'm going to pay her a little visit and bring her something shiny. She never could refuse a present, and this one shall be her unmaking. Zeren is in the thick of this war, but you shall send him this letter." Rahaxeris smoothed a fresh piece of parchment and began writing.

When he finished, he rolled it, sealed it, and handed it to her. "I don't care if you get covered in dirt and blood on the way. I want you to put that in Zeren's hand. *You*, not a messenger. Do that successfully, and the priests might allow you a little more time to live."

Zefyre bowed. "Yes, sir. Thank you." She turned and walked out of the *Rune-dy's* upper chamber, tears flowing silently from her eyes. The knowledge that her days were numbered infected her.

****

Once Zefyre was gone, Rahaxeris sat in quiet contemplation. It was time to call a meeting of the priests. The change of his plans would have to be approved by a majority vote. He had to sell the new idea to them. However, selling was a far cry from laying bare the truth. He was the leader, and they were on a need-to-know basis. He thought through the way he would inform them what he wanted without it seeming as though it was *his mere desire* but what was best for Regia.

He left the main room and walked down a long hallway to his personal chambers. He placed a hand on the circular light beam in the center of the luminous Belliss stone wall until it expanded, creating a doorway large enough for him to enter.

The room would have looked bare to an outsider, like an extra quest room in an unused part of the house. But as soon as the light closed the stone behind him, Rahaxeris' most secret and vulnerable memories filled the room like a family of ghosts. They emerged from the stone, wispy, transparent, and whispering their damnable truths.

He looked at Forest, the day she was born. As it always did, the love he had for his daughter stung deeply and weighed him down with guilt. Love kept secret, denied. *My child.* There was nothing tender in this emotion. It had teeth and claws and craved the blood of all who had harmed her.

Leith's face swirled in the haze before him. Rahaxeris' hands and teeth clenched. So long, he had waited to spill his blood. His restraint through the years almost killed him. Leith would pay. Christiana would pay. Both would burn in the fire of his retribution. Soon.

The memories dissipated like steam.

He retrieved the green stone he'd created the day before from its protected place in the wall and slipped it into his robes. He left his chambers and ventured lower underground to the metal stores. Only the best metal would do for the necklace he would make with the stone. Not the best metal that could be found in Regia, but the best metal in any world, anywhere. Moreover, it would be the most beautiful and powerful piece of jewelry he had ever made.

He stepped into the Worlds room and greeted Hezeron, who was bent over the corpse of a strange birdlike creature, focused intently on its dissection. He glanced up swiftly at Rahaxeris and nodded.

"Rahaxeris."

"Hezeron."

"What brings you here?" Hezeron asked.

"Metal, and I need a page out of The Book of Worlds."

"Help yourself."

Hezeron asked no questions about Rahaxeris' project. He merely continued to study his specimen in silence, occasionally glancing over at what Rahaxeris was doing. Only after Rahaxeris was finished and held the necklace up to inspect it did Hezeron give him his full attention.

"Superior work, sir. Your choice of Talereneain Firelight Silver does raise my curiosity as to the intended purpose of the piece."

"Why?" Rahaxeris asked calmly, never betraying the worry now crawling inside him.

"It must be important to you to use such a magical and precious metal."

"Not at all. I'm fond of the stone I created, and I thought the Firelight made the most attractive setting."

Hezeron gazed speculatively at the necklace. Rahaxeris slipped it into his pocket. "Its purpose shall be a topic at our next meeting. Now, I need The Book of Worlds."

Hezeron stood from the table and crossed the cavernous room to a wall of shelves. His long fingers caressed the spines of the books as he scanned the titles. A terrible screaming filled the room, no louder than a whisper. He gave the Soul Jar on the shelf above his head a sharp flick of his finger. The milky glass vibrated, and the screaming stopped.

"What is in there?" Rahaxeris asked gesturing to the jar as Hezeron brought him the heavy tome.

Hezeron smiled. "Oh, that's a rather foul tempered pixie I killed on my last trip to *Neverland*. I'm not sure what I'm going to do with her."

"Why don't you splice her into that bird-thing you've got there and see what happens?"

Hezeron raised one imperial eyebrow and looked down at the dissected remains. "Hmm... Maybe. So what are you looking for in there?" He pointed at the book.

"A good place to exile someone."

"Ah. Try chapter seven."

Rahaxeris thumbed through the book, until he found the perfect fit for Christiana. He felt killing Christiana was within his right as a father, but he knew torture was better. Being the leader of the *Rune-dy*, torture was in his nature and he was exceptionally gifted at it. Yet he couldn't torture Christiana as he would like to; time and circumstances prevented it. Permanent exile would have to suffice.

Rahaxeris tore the chosen page out and set the book carefully aside. He balled the parchment in his fist and closed his eyes. Flames engulfed his hand as he turned the piece of parchment into a trapdoor perfectly tailored for the queen.

Opening his hand, Rahaxeris examined the throbbing red jewel. It wasn't quite ready. Removing Christiana from the equation wasn't punishment enough. He pulled a single hair from his head and wound it around the jewel. The blond thread sank inside and took on the appearance of a vein of gold within the stone. He blew gently on the jewel and muttered a few carefully considered elvish words. With loving thoughts of his daughter and a small vindictive smile on his face, Rahaxeris set the red jewel into a simple gold chain. He tucked the necklace in beside the one he made for Forest. It was time to call the meeting.

He strode silently into the lab. Menjel was working and he hated being disturbed when he was in the lab. Rahaxeris wanted to grimace. Menjel looked like a butcher; blood spattered over his sleeves and apron. The excited light of new pain glinted in his ruby eyes. Whomever he had just been experimenting on was gone, leaving their blood on the operating table.

Menjel was making notes furiously on a diagram. "Come here, Rah, and look at this," he said.

Rahaxeris sighed at his use of an abbreviation for his name but said nothing. "What have you done?" He looked over Menjel's shoulder.

"I've created a new way to inject thoughts. My latest test, on an elf, worked perfectly. The injected thought made him believe he itched all over. He began to scratch his skin but the harder he scratched the stronger the itch became. It took roughly an hour, but the test victim tore all of his skin off."

"I see," Rahaxeris said approvingly. "Are you thinking of using this for interrogation or pre-death punishment?"

"Both. However, I cannot recommend it for interrogation until I figure out how to stop the sensation before the victim kills himself. Baal can work on that tomorrow."

"Fine. Clean up. We have a meeting."

"Yes, sir."

****

Rune-dy meetings never lasted very long. None of the priests were verbose. Since there were only seven of them and only two departments, there was hardly ever anything they didn't know about each other's work. Rahaxeris was thankful for their lack of curiosity today.

He sat at the end of the table with the heads of each department, Abshael and Cassian, closest to him. The senior levels, Menjel and Hezeron, were next, and then the assistants, Baal and Plixtz. Being the leader, Rahaxeris presided over every meeting.

He addressed the priests. "New business. Philippe is dead at the hand of an unsanctioned, sacrificial messenger sent by Zefyre."

Muttering erupted around the table.

"She must die!" Cassian said sternly.

Everyone nodded in agreement.

"Yes, yes," Rahaxeris said unconcernedly. "That is of little concern. The real problem is the balance was disrupted by Philippe dying before we intended him to."

"Zeren is weak. We can make him our puppet," Hezeron added.

Rahaxeris smiled inside. Hezeron had handed him the perfect launching point. "Yes, Zeren is weak, but Christiana is not." He pulled the red-jeweled necklace from his robes and placed it on the table where everyone could see. "I want to exile her."

"Why?" Menjel demanded. "She's no obstacle."

"She's been trying to kill Forest."

"Oh, well..." Menjel crossed his arms across his chest. "I thought we all agreed not to interfere with our little pet."

Everyone at the table leaned in a little. All of them had watched Forest's progress since infancy. And they all had voted to allow her to live, even after they had collected all the data they wanted about her gifts. None of the other Halflings that had been created in that experiment were still alive.

"Oh, let him do what he wants to Christiana," Plixtz sounded bored.

"All in favor of exile for Christiana?"

Everyone raised their hands.

"Now, since our original plan has been ruined by Philippe's death, we must adapt. Once Christiana is gone, ripping the kingdom away from Zeren will be easy." Rahaxeris pulled the green-jeweled necklace from his robes and held it up for the priests to see. "I want to create a position of supreme judge for the new republic. A title only for those who cannot be bought or corrupted with power. The title of *Hailemarris*."

"Who do you have in mind for such a position?" Abshael asked.

"No one yet," he lied.

Chapter Four

A nervous sweat beaded on the face of the young male servant who received Rahaxeris into the entry hall of the Onyx Castle. Rahaxeris doubted the boy knew his actual identity but he obviously recognized him as a priest of the *Rune-dy*.

"My sincerest apologies, sir," the servant muttered. "It will take me only a moment to inform Her Highness that you are here." He literally ran from the room, his footsteps echoing along after him.

Rahaxeris stood perfectly still while he waited. The security ogres positioned around the room all seemed to hold their breath and stiffen a little more in their stances. Rahaxeris ignored them completely. He couldn't be bothered to attempt to put others at ease.

He eyed the grandeur of the room's architecture thoughtfully. In the very recent past, he'd had a mind to tear every stone of the palace apart once the new world order had settled firmly into place. Now that his plans were altered, he consoled himself with the thought *his* daughter would walk these halls as its mistress.

Running footfalls came sounding back through the hall. Thirty feet from the door, the young man slowed to a walk and emerged into the entry hall with the determined look of false composure. "The Queen will see you now, sir. Please follow me."

When Rahaxeris entered the throne room, an audible gasp communally escaped every handmaiden and servant. Queen Christiana's rigid posture betrayed her obvious effort to appear unshaken, and to her credit almost pulled it off. She sat in Zeren's throne, so overdressed she resembled a little girl in a costume.

"So, why does the *Rune-dy* send a priest for an audience with the queen?"

Rahaxeris might have smiled if it weren't for the fact that he never did unless he wanted to terrify someone. "My Queen, the *Rune-dy* has not sent me. *I am* the *Rune-dy*. I am Rahaxeris."

A louder gasp than before erupted around the room, and the servants closest to the doors exited without permission. The others backed away and huddled in groups against the walls. Christiana glanced at them, a furious expression on her little face.

Rahaxeris held up a hand, and everyone stopped breathing, literally. "What I have come to say to Her Majesty is best said in private. Perhaps you should send your guards and servants away. That one there," he pointed at a shaking handmaiden, "is having heart palpitations and on the verge of passing out."

Christiana raised an eyebrow. "How do you know she is having palpitations?"

"I can hear it. Now dismiss them so I can speak."

Christiana obeyed, obviously annoyed at having no other choice. When the Ogres made to leave, she stopped them. "Stay right outside the doors."

Once the room was empty and the echo of the closing doors had died, Rahaxeris regarded her silently for a moment. Again to her credit, she didn't fidget, but all the blood had drained from her face and her muscles began to slacken as his red eyes held her in a tight grip.

"I have come to speak to you of the future and to make a secret alliance."

He felt her heart pick up a little speed, and she clenched her fists. "Go on."

"Zeren is weak. You, my lady, are anything but. Regia is hanging in the balance. Our world needs a strong leader. The *right* leader. The *Rune-dy* is willing to support your claim to Zeren's throne and power."

"I agree." She all but squealed in delight. "Are you going to kill Zeren?"

"In good time, My Queen. First we must seal our contract."

She stood, her skirts spreading out around her. "Fine. What are the terms?"

"The *Rune-dy* will support your rule throughout Regia and set the punishment for traitors. You shall not interfere in any of our secret rituals or lay down laws preventing our experiments. A couple of priests will take up residence in the Onyx Castle as your personal advisors."

Christiana's eyes widened and her breath caught audibly. Pleasure glinted in her eyes. He knew she would like the idea of the *Rune-dy* in the castle.

"Zeren shall fall in battle, allowing the public to easily embrace you in their time of confusion and sorrow."

"Yes, yes that is best," she said.

"We shall complete our contract in the ancient way, with an exchange of tokens."

A frown creased Christiana's brow. "What token have you brought me?"

Rahaxeris reached into his robes and removed the red-jeweled necklace. He dangled it from his fingers for her to see. A broad smile broke over her face.

"It is not merely a piece of jewelry, my lady. It grants protection and power to the wearer. Having this around your neck, no underlings will ever be able to argue with you."

Her eyes fixed on it greedily. Rahaxeris moved closer, bringing the necklace just beyond her reach. She held out her hand.

"Not so fast."

"What do you want in return?" She asked not taking her eyes off the necklace.

"In order to receive this token you must give me your son."

Christiana blinked and looked back at Rahaxeris, a false puzzlement on her face. "My son? My son is dead."

"You may be skilled in deception, my lady, but do you really think you can lie to *me*?"

"It's the truth! I know you know that he survived that assassination attempt five years ago, but he just recently died on a mission to regain his sight."

Rahaxeris sighed and slowly began to put the necklace back into his robes.

"No! Wait! What do you want with Syrus? He's not well. His mind has been bewitched."

"If that is true, why not trust me to heal him?"

"I thought you meant to dispatch him along with his father."

"I mean him no harm," Rahaxeris said easily, dangling the necklace again.

Christiana hesitated a moment. "The ogre, Merhl, is the only one who can open the portal to Syrus. Shall I summon him?"

"No. That won't be necessary. Allow me to fasten this around your neck, my lady. Then our contract will be struck."

Christiana pulled her dark hair up off her shoulders and bowed her head a little. As soon as Rahaxeris brought the two ends of the chain together, the reaction began. He took a step back, enjoying the frozen look of shock and fear in her eyes. The red jewel glowed bright and encased her in a glassy cocoon of energy. She began to blur around the edges. The power held her immobile, staring.

"No doubt you are wondering what you could have done to deserve this kind of double crossing. Your son's mate, Forest, is my daughter. I am allowing you to live out your life, confined in another world, with the knowledge that Forest shall sit on your throne."

Rahaxeris took a few more steps back and watched as Christiana faded into nothing. He waited a few silent moments before beginning the task of taking control of the castle and everyone within. He pulled his power inside and held it there like inhaling. It gathered, compacted, vibrated. Eyes closed, exhaling slowly, his power radiated out from him like a shockwave, filling the walls and the hearts of every inhabitant.

He strolled out from the throne room; everyone he passed bowed in submission.

"I seek the ogre, Merhl," he said loudly.

Merhl walked demurely and bowed before Rahaxeris. He was younger and smaller than most of the ogres lining the walls, but power emanated from him. Rahaxeris' power recognized and analyzed Merhl's. He was the most gifted ogre Rahaxeris had ever met. His skin was a mottled bronze and grey. His dark hair was shortly cropped and matched the color of his eyes. Merhl's gifts resided predominantly in his hands, and had the same effects of genius; it caused him as much pain as it did pleasure. His massive hands were elongated and twisted, and anyone could see they ached fiercely. Rahaxeris liked Merhl instantly.

"Give me your hands."

Merhl flinched in fear but obeyed.

Rahaxeris gripped both of Merhl's disfigured hands. The power throbbed just under the ogre's skin. Rahaxeris syphoned off the excess magic. Merhl's eyes snapped wide and a smile flashed across his face.

"There. That's better isn't it?"

"Yes, sir. Thank you."

"It helps the pain when you are allowed to use your gifts frequently?"

"Yes, sir."

"Good. I have many jobs for you, Merhl. Now take me to Prince Syrus."

Impressed, Rahaxeris ran his hand over the exterior of the portal that held Syrus. Merhl stood next to him with his eyes on the ground, clenching and unclenching his hands.

"Well done, Merhl. It's a beautiful prison. I'd like to keep it. Can you fix it after I break it open?"

"I can, of course, sir, but…"

"But what?"

Merhl wrung his hands together. "But I'd rather just make you a new one."

Rahaxeris almost smiled. "Very well. When we are done with the prince, I want you to create a vacuum that will suck all the vampires roaming illegally on Earth back to Regia. Can you do that?"

Merhl's eyes lit with excitement. "It would be my pleasure."

****

After three months of complete silence, the breaking of the cell was excruciatingly loud. A hand reached inside, grabbed Syrus by the forearm, and pulled him back into the world from the abyss. He came out fighting, adrenaline pushing strength back into his muscles.

"Where is she?! Where is she?!"

Syrus had a death grip on Rahaxeris' shoulders. Rahaxeris deftly removed Syrus' hands and held them in his own. He sent a calming wave of energy into Syrus.

"Forest is on Earth. You will be able to see her again very shortly."

Syrus checked himself, recognizing that he confronted a stranger. "Who are you?"

"I am Rahaxeris, High Priest of the *Rune-dy*, but more importantly, I am Forest's father."

Syrus pulled his hands free and took a step back. "You're exactly what she feared."

"I doubt that."

"What is your purpose here?" Syrus demanded. "Why are you the one who released me?"

"Your father is in battle, and your mother has made many attempts to kill Forest since she imprisoned you. I had to step in."

Syrus gritted his teeth and took a deep breath. "What did you do with my mother?"

"I banished Christiana to the lovely little world of Brigadoon. She won't be able to return."

Mixed emotions moved over Syrus' features for a moment before settling on a mix of relief and resignation.

"Thank you. I want to talk to you at length, but right now I need to get Forest and bring her home to Regia."

Rahaxeris smiled. "Of course. I'll have Merhl open a portal to Forest's abode for you."

****

The portal transporting Syrus to Forest's condo only took a few seconds, but it was too slow for his taste. He landed on his feet in her living room.

"Forest! Forest!"

There was no answer.

"Forest!"

She wasn't there. The place was empty. Syrus had never before been crushed with such disappointment. He took a deep breath, Forest's scent filling his lungs. Oh, to smell her was such torture. After the months of isolation, being so close to his desire and still not grasping it, crippled him with an even greater longing.

He paced, running his hands over every surface.

Chapter Five

Forest's vision tunneled around Pandora's apartment door. For the third time, she reached into her pocket and pulled out the piece of paper with the address written on it. This was the place. The noise of people splashing in the pool around the corner added to the rushing in Forest's ears. Adrenaline spiked her blood pressure. This was going to be it. She could feel it. This was the last time. She would kill Leith and finally be free. Sweat ran down her body under her clothes and moistened the metal against her skin. She had burned Leith with silver before, but today she would do it thoroughly.

Forest barely stopped herself from kicking in the door. He was probably sleeping. If she could slip in quietly, she could have the pleasure of waking him from his dreams into a bloody nightmare of her own making. The thought gave her a sexual thrill.

The door was unlocked. She entered the darkened apartment and slipped the deadbolt behind her. She didn't move or breathe while her eyes adjusted to the dimness. Leith was asleep on the couch.

Forest made a full assessment of her surroundings. The small one-bedroom apartment gave him no escape unless he wanted to go out into the sun. The fool had trapped himself in a little box, caged inside by the daylight. She moved silently into the one-butt kitchen. There wasn't much there except empty pizza boxes and a pile of dirty dishes in the sink that were becoming sentient. Clothes littered the chip-crumb covered carpet.

She watched his chest rise and fall a few times. She could just slit his throat while he slept, but that felt too impersonal. She wanted to draw it out. Her first idea had been to find a rolling pin, but after looking through every inch of the tiny kitchen, discovered there was none. She settled with the sole frying pan and was grateful it was clean. She strode over to him and straddled him. He sighed in his sleep and his eyes fluttered. Forest leaned down and kissed his mouth roughly. He awoke faster than she had anticipated and wrapped his arms around her back. She watched his eyes open as he filled her mouth with his tongue. Forest pulled back as far as he would let her. She had no idea what she looked like but she saw recognition in his eyes.

"It's been a while, Forest. I've been missing you."

Forest smiled broadly. "Hello, lover."

The pan raping smartly on the top of his head made a wonderfully comical sound. Forest envisioned little birds flying around his unconscious head. The months of built up stress came pouring out of her in loud maniacal cackling. For the very first time, she had the upper hand with Leith.

Forest hefted Leith into a green, third-hand recliner and secured him to it with an entire roll of duct tape. She sat on the floor and toyed with the last piece of tape she'd saved to cover his mouth and regarded him thoughtfully. Her tormentor, her master, her lover. She could feel the difference inside her since she had last seen him. Forest had no doubt Syrus was the cause. Leith's hold on her had never been weaker. Even so, the wisest thing for her to do was to gag him before she woke him, but she didn't want to.

His head lolled on his shoulder. It was hard to feel violent toward him when he was helpless. She cursed herself and him that she was conflicted at all.

She balled the tape and dropped it, then gazed at him intently. He was so beautiful on the outside. *That's about to change.* She ran her fingers down her scars then pulled a silver chain from her pocket.

Forest approached him and slapped him in the face as hard as she could. The burning sting through her hand was well worth it.

Leith's eyes sprang open and locked on her. He strained against the tape. "Forest, you will let me out of this binding right now!" he ordered.

Forest exhaled the breath she'd been holding. The pull to obey was there, but she defied it. Her scars burned and pulled in response to her disobedience.

She smiled. "No. I don't think so."

He blinked at her stupidly for a moment. "I said, let me out!" he pronounced each word harshly.

Her smile stretched a little wider. "*I said no.*"

"What has happened, Forest? What have you *done*?" He narrowed his eyes. His face mirrored his thoughts as he sifted through them. Red colored his cheeks, and his eyes bugged as he stared. "Someone else has had their hands on you! Haven't they?" he roared.

Forest clapped for him. "Bravo! I'm impressed, Leith. You really aren't as stupid as you look."

Leith ground his teeth together, straining against the tape, blood vessels breaking in his eyes.

She twirled the silver chain in her hand where he could see it. "Pipe down."

"*You faithless Halfling, half-breed, mixed blood, hybrid!* How dare you? You're *mine*. You've always been mine! You'll always be mine! I own you!"

The instinct to cower, to beg, and apologize pulled at her.

"Who is he?" Leith demanded.

She ignored the question.

Leith laughed humorlessly. "A filthy werewolf, I'll bet. No! No, a human. You ensnared a human with your witchy eyes."

Forest refused to be baited. "Are you ready to die?" she asked calmly.

Leith changed tact. "Forest, I love you! Don't you know that? No one else loves you. No one else could love a Halfling like you. I marked you to put you under my protection. I knew how unkind the world would be to you. I had to shield you. Whomever this person is that you've tricked into being your lover will hate you once they learn the truth about you. He'll leave you. Forget him. Let me loose and we'll reaffirm our love. We'll go back to Regia together. We can go public. I'll let everyone know, I promise. I know you've wanted that."

An unexpected pain sliced through Forest at his words. Had she ever wanted that? She knew clearly there was nothing she wanted now more than to be with Syrus. But what about before she met Syrus? Leith had used the word *love* many times, usually after inflicting pain. But if he had ever used it and meant it, what would she have done? After everything that happened and everything he had done to her, could she have forgiven him?

She mentally slapped herself. All blinders fell from her eyes and locked on Leith's. There was nothing there to salvage. Her heart had expired long ago where Leith was concerned. It was time to move on. Leith compared to Syrus was like choosing a busted old lemon over a brand new Mercedes AMG.

"There's nothing I want from you, except your death."

The fear of God came into his eyes. "No please, don't kill me, Forest! You're better than me. After everything we've shared—"

"Don't go there!"

"I'm sorry. My methods of love were wrong. I didn't know another way. I had a bad childhood. My father was harsh on me. Forgive me. Please, Forest, I'm sorry."

"It's too late for those words, Leith. They mean nothing to me."

She moved in. Leith began to sob loudly. She wished now she had kept the tape.

She looked around and picked up a tank top from the stuff strewn across the floor and shoved the fabric into Leith's mouth. His eyes bulged, and he let out a muffled scream of pain as Forest jerked his head to the side and laid the silver chain on his neck in exactly the same place her scars began. The stench of his burning flesh filled her nose. She worked slowly, intending to recreate the look of her scars on his skin.

She reached the collar of his shirt, pulled out a pocketknife to cut away the fabric, and then he was gone. Vanished into thin air right under her hands, leaving the chair covered in torn tape. Forest jumped back, her mind tripping. *What just happened? No! No! NO!!!*

Forest screamed and threw the chair across the room, breaking a lamp. Why? Why was fate so cruel to her?

She focused on her breathing. What was going on in Regia? Something was happening. She picked up the busted chair and put it back where it had been. Tears of fury rolled down her cheeks as she dropped two hundred dollars on the counter to cover the cost of damages and left.

She drove recklessly through Austin with no destination in mind. Zigzagging through traffic, she let the roar of the Demon's engine soothe her. She drove all the way to Huston before turning around and going home.

The lights of the city punched holes in the blue velvet darkness. When Forest pulled into her one-car garage, she was hungry and tired and felt as if she'd been beat up. It hadn't been the very worst day of her life but it definitely made the top five. She had to try to find out what was going on in Regia. Maybe after dinner she'd call Kindel.

She entered her condo, locked the door behind her, hung her bag on the doorknob, and froze. Her nostrils flared. There was a vampire behind her.

Forest spun around, pulling her magnum out of her waistband, her arm snapping straight out, the barrel of the gun one inch from the sucker's face.

The whole world flipped and the gun slipped from her hand. "OH!" She sobbed. "Syrus!"

Three months of separation, of her heart strained, pulled and twisted caused the first moment of release to explode in a stronger screaming sting, delivering more pain than she had yet experienced. She forced herself to breathe while the spiritual bond between them sparked and spluttered like a damp candlewick before blazing bright. The invisible cords connecting them vibrated and shimmered in light, heat, and color.

Syrus' black pearl eyes were open, staring at her. Locking gazes with Syrus was like a punch to the brain. A sharp little fist that delivered a snap of pain then extended its fingers out, stroking her mind with soft ecstasy. She reached slowly for his face. Her fingers stopped an inch from his cheek. "Is it really you?" she whispered, afraid. "Am I dreaming?"

His whole body trembled as he reached up and took hold of her hand. "Am *I*?" he asked. His breath caught as he pressed her palm against his cheek. This first contact seared like a burn then sang like a breeze. The connection roared within them tearing at their insides, demanding more.

Forest jumped, threading herself tightly around him. Breathing became easier than it had been since she'd been banished, even with her mouth fused to his. Frenzied and trying to absorb each other. And still the connection screamed, *More!*

"I love you, Syrus!" She managed between kisses.

"I love you, Forest!"

"What happened to you? How did you get here? Are you okay? Were you hurt?"

He placed his finger gently over her lips. "Shh. We'll talk later."

"Why not now?"

"It's really hot in here, Forest. You might want to do something to lower the temperature."

"Oh?"

"It's about to get a lot hotter."

She managed to knock her elbow into the thermostat, turning up the AC, as they made their way haphazardly into the bedroom. It was a good thing she did too.

I'm burning, Syrus! You set my soul on fire. And when it burns down to nothing, I'll be yours completely.

With tears, breath, skin, lips, and hearts they shattered each other.

****

Forest awoke hours later, rested, sated, and spiritually peaceful. Her head pillowed on Syrus' arm, she gazed into his sleeping face. She had so many questions, but none of them mattered now. She placed her hand on his chest, feeling the beating of his heart. *Nothing matters but this.*

He stirred under her touch and yawned. Syrus opened his eyes. His pupils had closed again. He caressed her face gently. "Forest." He said her name reverently.

He pulled her tightly against him and kissed her. She thought back a few hours; she could definitely handle some more of that. It had been so very different from anything she'd ever experienced before. There was no pain, no damage to her body or soul. Just love and trust, absolute trust. Syrus didn't take, he gave. Warm shivers rolled through her body then Syrus abruptly pulled away.

"Hey!" she protested. "Come back here."

He laughed, getting off the bed. "Where are my clothes?"

"*Really?* You want to get dressed?"

"Not at all," he chuckled. "I need my flask. It's on my belt."

Forest sat up and looked at the mess of clothes on her floor. "To your right."

He grabbed the belt from the floor and pulled his flask off. She winced as he took a swig. Tears burned her eyes as he cringed and growled in pain. It only took a moment, but every second of his pain ripped through her.

Syrus straightened his shoulders, took a few deep breaths, and then opened his eyes.

"Why would you do that to yourself?"

Syrus raised one eyebrow. "You're naked."

She gave a little yelp as he grabbed the edge of the sheet and jerked it off the bed.

"So," she said saucily. "You'd go through that kind of pain just to ogle me?"

"Obviously."

"Was it worth it?...Syrus?"

"Huh? I'm sorry what did you say?"

Forest laughed, shaking her head. "Come back here."

Forest awoke in the dark, hours later. Light from the street lamps outside pushed through the fabric of her curtains. The small amount of light made everything in the room a silhouette. Her head rested on Syrus' chest, and his hand skimmed up and down her scars lightly. She didn't like that and was instantly self-conscious.

"Stop that," she ordered, moving her shoulder away.

He gripped both her shoulders and rolled her under him, his fingers digging deep into her flesh. Teeth flashed in the darkness before her eyes.

"Faithless whore! I'll teach you who you belong to," Leith snarled.

Forest screamed as Leith sank his teeth into the tangle of her scars. Her flesh tore and burned between his teeth.

Syrus held Forest in the circle of his arms while she slept. He couldn't sleep anymore but was content laying still, replaying the last hours in his mind. He didn't want to disturb her slumber but couldn't stop himself from pressing his lips into her hair or brushing them across her temple every so often. After all the pain of separation, being together this way, completely, was a marvel. *She* was a marvel, and the love he had for her filled him up and stretched outward beyond his flesh, imbuing his aura with intense golden light.

He exhaled, and his thoughts moved to the future, *their* future, then she suddenly stiffened in his arms. Her whole body went rigid, and a strangled cry escaped her lips. Knowing all too well how violently she could wake up, Syrus pulled her closer and whispered, "I'm here, Forest. It's Syrus. There's no one here but me. Just Syrus."

She cried out again, her body jerking, her arms and legs flailing. Syrus let go and rolled away from her. "Wake up, Forest!" he commanded loudly now.

"I am awake," she rasped. Her body bucked and cringed, and she screamed in agony.

"What's happening? What can I do?" He was desperate.

"It burns! It burns so bad!" she cried. "No! Don't touch me!"

She groped for her bedside lamp and turned it on. The pain was so terrible she wished she had something to bite down on. Her eyes tried to focus on her scars. The crescent lovers marks glowed bright red, like coals in a fire. Then starting at the top, one by one, they tore open and bled. Forest pushed past Syrus and ran into the bathroom. She turned the faucet on and splashed water on her arm.

Syrus was on her heels. She slammed the door and locked it.

"Forest what's happening?!" He shouted, panic woven through his voice.

"I'm all right. Just give me a minute."

He leaned his head against the door, teeth clenched, and tried to slow his breathing. She had been or was still in some intense pain and yet he couldn't feel it. Their connection should have alerted him to what she was going through, but he could sense nothing. His heart felt the beating of hers, her vital signs were strong and steady. Whatever she was experiencing was outside of the entity that was "them."

Then the knowledge of the cause ran through his blood like poison. *Leith.*

The physical price of consummating their connection while she was under Leith's power was uncharted territory. Syrus might have been able to consider there would be ramifications for her, if they hadn't been separated so long. But there were no thoughts in his head once he arrived in her apartment. He waited for her to return. Surrounded by her things, inundated by her scent. No, there were no thoughts when she came through the door. The connection took over both of them and brought them to completion. He was far from sorry. But now Forest was suffering something he couldn't stop, fix, or ease.

He scrubbed his hands over his face and walked back to the bedroom. He pulled his pants on and sat down on the edge of the bed, turning his flask around in his hands. Should he take another drink? Did he need his sight or his strength more at this moment? Syrus punched the mattress. *Damn it all to hell.* He flipped the lid open and took a drink, fighting back the involuntary cry of pain in his throat as his eyes tore themselves open. If she was in pain, then he would be in pain, too.

The sound of the bathroom door opening had Syrus on his feet. Forest walked slowly around the corner, into his line of sight. He couldn't read her expression. Tears ran freely down her cheeks. She stood still, facing him, her whole body taut as a wire.

"Forest, what is it? What's wrong?"

"Well...uh...it..." she stumbled over her words, her face slack.

The next second her smile lit up the whole room and she squealed, jumping at him.

"LOOK!" She cried. "Look, look, look! They're gone, Syrus! GONE!"

"What's gone?"

"The marks! The lovers marks are gone!"

She thrust her upper arm toward his face. He looked closely at her skin. The straight line—the slave mark was still there, but the seven crescent lover's marks were gone. Her skin was pink, as though it had been roughly scrubbed.

"Oh look...my skin...gone...all gone..." Forest's words came out in jerky sobs, and she collapsed against Syrus, weeping uncontrollably.

He held her tightly, tears blurring his eyes as well.

"I'm half-free."

Syrus cupped her face in his hands and kissed her fiercely.

She took a deep breath, steadying the spasms in her lungs. "Oh, Syrus, I've never been so happy in my entire life. These last few hours... ever since you got here...have been so wonderful, like a miracle even. And now half of my scars are gone." Her voice broke again. "I love you so much!"

"I love you, too. More than I ever knew to be possible."

Chapter Six

Shi hovered over Netriet as she slept, infusing her cells with energy pulled from The Heart. She was bemused at herself, not quite sure why she cared so much that this young vampire live. She considered Netriet's character equally split between good and bad. She had never saved the life of a vampire before. Maybe it was the novelty of the action that spurred her on, or possibly, it was her lack of having anything else to do. The Wood was now completely devoid of werewolves, now they had all marched off to war.

Netriet moaned as Shi knit one of her broken ribs back together. Shi kept her in a deep sleep at all times so she wouldn't have to experience any more pain. She smiled unwittingly at the vampire. Netriet's courage and strength reminded her of Forest.

She killed Philippe. I'd grow her a new arm for that if I could.

Shi flew back to The Heart and cupped her insubstantial hands in the black flames of the manifestation. A small tongue of fire alighted on her palms. She took it back to Netriet. Slowly, Shi pushed her ghostly hands through the skin of Netriet's stomach; the fire rebuilt the walls of her interior organs.

A few more hours in her care, and Netriet would be better than new. Much better. Shi smiled as she imagined how happy and amazed Netriet would be when she woke up and found she was so much…so much…better? Superior? A shadow of doubt crept into the periphery of Shi's mind as she flew back to the Heart. She reached in again and brought a small tongue of flame close to her face. The Heart was black. The world was filled with dark emotion. What was that doing to Netriet? The power was healing her body, but what was it doing to her spirit? Her psyche?

Shi brought the fire back to Netriet and sat down next to her. She toyed with the flame for a few moments. How many times had she infused it into the young woman? Could she remove it? Not without killing her. Should she kill her? What kind of monster was she creating? Would it have been a better kindness to have let her die?

As she contemplated ending Netriet's life, she realized she didn't have the heart for it. She would monitor her before releasing her back into the world. Shi looked closely at Netriet's sleeping face, and an emotion she hadn't felt for centuries darkened her…fear.

What have I done?

Shi stayed next to Netriet for days and waited for her healing to complete. Slowly, she began to bring her closer to the surface of waking. She began gathering things the werewolves had left lying around, thinking Netriet might need them when she made her way back out into the world. She fought against the desire to hold Netriet captive once she was awake. She wouldn't be the right kind of mentor the young woman needed. She would have to find her own way, decide right or wrong on her own. And despite her longing for company, Shi decided to move Netriet outside The Wood before she woke.

A few hours later, invisible in the branches overhead, Shi watched Netriet regain consciousness, instantly alarmed as the vampire opened her eyes. Her left eye was different. A smoky black tentacle snaked through her amber iris and wound a circle around her pupil. She could see the shadows veining through Netriet's heart, pushing deeper with each beat.

****

Awareness moved slowly, rising from the darkness. Netriet memories smeared together like modern art. She knew her name, where she was born, and the faces of her parents. Most memories were intact, but in her drowsy, semi-conscious state, she found her feelings skewed. The way she had always felt about certain things changed.

Netriet opened her eyes slowly. A canopy of branches stretched out overhead, blocking the morning sunlight. *How did I get here?* The tilting sky as she fell, clasped to Philippe's chest, came back to her mind. *I was dead.*

She sat up, surveying her surroundings, groping for her missing arm. Her fingers clutched a sleeve tied into a knot. These were not the clothes she had died in. Simple clothes that fit well enough and smelled like werewolf. She wiggled her toes in the too-big shoes. A lumpy pack sat next to her leg. She opened it. Food, water, a knife, and a change of clothes.

The transparent being. Shi's eyes and voice came back to Netriet like the remnant of a dream. What had she done?

Netriet looked more closely at things. She held her hand up to her face, contracting and extending her fingers. Black scars laced the edge of her hand and ran down her wrist. Netriet looked at the contrasting color confusedly, suddenly worried about just how scarred her face might be and if it was lined with black as well.

She ran her fingertips lightly over her face. The ridge of a scar wound a jagged line next to her hairline and another on the temple by her right eye. Tears sprang to her eyes. The injustice of what had happened to her and what she had been reduced to, pulled down like gravity. She wrapped her arm around her knees and wept bitterly. What was she to do? Where could she go? Was there anywhere that would welcome a creature like her?

Netriet cried until her sorrow and self-pity were spent. Then something darker spread inside her, just under the skin. She raised her head, startled as if someone or something had called her name. And indeed, something had. Something inside her, another entity, unreasoning, volatile, and solely emotional.

Netriet struggled to her feet, picked up the pack, and slung it across her body. She eyed The Wood behind her dubiously. She had died in there and now she was…transformed. She had no desire to go back and investigate. She didn't give a damn for answers or excuses, if the transparent being would even give her any. Anger and blame clutched at her throat.

She looked out on the world ahead. Where would she go?

Did it matter? She was alive. Regardless of what she felt or wanted, she had to reinvent herself. She could shed her name and make up a story about how she lost her arm.

Netriet straightened her spine. She extended her fingers and contracted them into a fist. She would survive. She would carve out a future with her one hand.

****

Rahaxeris leaned back lazily in the throne, his sharp fingers drumming on the armrests. He didn't care for it. However, it was still necessary to make a show of his authority to everyone in the castle. If he was correct in his calculations—and he always was—Zeren would be arriving shortly, in a fit no doubt. He contemplated the outcome of his time with Zeren. Maybe Zefyre's missteps would work out for the better: perhaps not for the better of Regia as a whole, but better for Forest. He could be content with that.

Rahaxeris could feel the moment of the King's arrival approaching. "Everyone leave the throne room," he ordered.

The handful of courtiers who had been reduced to fearful wallflowers obeyed immediately with obvious relief. Only Merhl hesitated. Rahaxeris nodded that he should leave as well.

The portal burst into the middle of the room. Zeren charged out of it, followed closely by Redge. Zeren drew his sword, locking his eyes on Rahaxeris. Rahaxeris flicked his finger, sending out a wave of grey energy that formed a transparent barrier to block Zeren.

Zeren, arrayed in his battle armor and half covered in mud, roared and struck the force field with his sword. The energy vibrated momentarily then smoothed out, unharmed.

"How dare you?!" Zeren shouted. "By what right have you routed my castle?"

Rahaxeris stood. "By my right as a parent."

His words made no sense to Zeren. "What did you say? Where is Christiana?"

"Speaking of the queen, tell me, Your Majesty, is royalty above the law?"

Zeren's brow furrowed as he contemplated his odd situation and took a calming breath. "No. Royalty is not above the law," he said uneasily.

"Then we are in agreement. I acted within the confines of the law, was lenient even, when I dispatched Queen Christiana to another realm. The law allows a person the right to protect the life of their child if persons or an individual threatens it, by any means. And since you charged off to war, Christiana has made unjustified, daily attempts to kill my daughter, Forest."

"Forest? The Halfling?"

"Correct."

"*She's* your daughter?" Zeren asked incredulously.

"And your daughter as well."

"I'm sorry, what was that?"

"Our children are destined life mates."

Zeren sheathed his sword and scrubbed a hand over his face. "Leave us, Redge."

Redge bowed and left the throne room. The eavesdroppers outside the doors instantly accosted him.

"What happened?"

"Did that *Rune-dy* say what he did to the queen?"

"What's happening on the battlefield?"

"What is the king going to do about all this?"

"What's going to happen to us if that elf kills the king?"

Redge stretched his arms out and began walking, gathering and pushing the people in front of him.

"Move along, you great idiots," Redge ordered. "That elf would kill you in a heartbeat for listening at the door. Don't you think he knew you were there anyway?"

The entire group gasped at once and scattered down the halls.

Redge clanked down the hall in his full armor, anxious to shed it. Making his way to his apartments, loosening the clasps of his vambraces, he caught sight of Merhl, pacing a small circuit and wringing his hands.

"Hey, Merhl."

The ogre glanced up nervously.

"Come and talk to me," Redge said.

****

Zeren paced and pulled at his armor as he listened to Rahaxeris talk. Processing his feelings wasn't easy. The world was flipping upside down. He had no way of knowing if what he was hearing was the truth.

"Okay. Hold it," Zeren said stopping Rahaxeris mid-sentence. "I'm going to need some time to think about all of this and to consult with my advisors about the legality."

"I understand that I have unloaded a lot of unexpected news on you, but you have apparently misunderstood one vital thing. I'm not giving you a choice."

"Now wait one damn minute. That's my throne you're sitting on."

"Not anymore."

The two men glared at each other, neither giving an inch.

After a moment, Rahaxeris' face relaxed. "I'm not your enemy, Zeren. Everything I have done, every bit of scheming, killing, and double-dealing has been for my daughter. I've set the world on fire to make it new, for her. It never occurred to me that her destined life mate would be someone of such consequence. Despite all I have done to make a better world for her, I never intended to place her on this throne." He gestured to Christiana's place next to him. "But she is in the position to take it if she chooses."

"I guess she is," Zeren conceded vaguely.

"You want Syrus to be king, don't you?"

"Yes! Very much. I'm just not sure… what with all that has happened and everything you've told me…" Zeren narrowed his eyes at Rahaxeris. "Would you allow Syrus to become king?"

"The *Rune-dy* is passionate about turning Regia into a republic. However, personally, I want my child to be happy above anything else. If Forest desires to be queen, I will allow it."

Zeren stared at him, calculating. "All right. Let's leave it up to them. The future of Regia is theirs anyway. They can decide its fate."

"I agree."

"So where are they?" Zeren asked.

"Earth. I assume they are enjoying their new connection. Forest has had enough hardship in her life. I don't intend to call them home before they are ready to return. "

"Okay. What do we do in the meantime?"

Rahaxeris gave Zeren a half smile. "We crush the Werewolves' pride and end the war."

The foundations of Zeren's whole life swirled and he hesitated *throwing his hat over the fence* until he had more time to consider and test the individual in front of him. Major decisions made in the midst of crisis and chaos never set well with him. Zeren was certain Syrus was able to face any challenge but he'd been through so much. And now he'd found his mate, she'd bring new things to the table and already had in the form of a powerful and frightening father.

Zeren nodded in agreement to Rahaxeris, while holding his reservations close to his chest.

Chapter Seven

Leith shook his head, disoriented. Were the effects of human blood making him insane? The pain of the silver burns on his neck felt like a knife wound, the blade still deep in his flesh. The blinding rage of Forest's disobedience and faithlessness mixed with his crippling fear of death. She was going to kill him. And yet, here he was, in the central marketplace of Halussis, surrounded by a large, disheveled group of fellow vampires, looking as flummoxed as he was.

"All right! All of you get in line. Get in line, I said!"

Leith looked around to see who was shouting orders. A stocky official climbed up on a planter. He scowled down at the motley bunch, papers and stylus in hand. A couple of ogres stood a ways behind him like oversized bouncers.

"Get in line!" he barked again.

"Yeah, and what if we don't, you little…squat…" The vampire striding up to the official staggered and slurred as though drunk. "…toad."

"Yeah?" a few more chimed in. "What are you gonna do, little man?"

The round faced official smiled down at the jeerer for a second then poked him smartly in the eye. The vampire stumbled backward, howling in pain, holding his hands over his face.

"Now, I know all of you are not in control of your senses, and you will start to rage soon for your addiction to human blood. You cannot go back to Earth. The portals have been shut. Line up and I shall take down your names before sending you off to rehab."

"This is an outrage!" an imperious voice rang out from the crowd. "Do you know who I am? I demand a royal escort to the castle at once."

The official snapped his fingers, and one of the ogres pushed through the crowd to the one making the fuss. Leith stood on his toes. The haughty vamp making demands was Dracula.

"How dare you!" Dracula yelled as the ogre picked him up. "Unhand me! I am Dracula! DRACULA! Put me down!"

The ogre looked back to the official. "It is Dracula, sir."

The official huffed and rolled his eyes. "Let him go back to the castle. He'll be wishing he stayed with us once he gets there."

The ogre dropped Dracula back on his feet. Leith pushed through the crowd. "Wait! Me too! I'm going with Dracula." Leith grabbed a hold of Dracula's arm.

"Oh no you don't!" the official barked. "Get in line."

"Please! I'm a noble."

Dracula sneered at Leith and jerked his arm loose.

"Dracula, please. It's me, Leith. Son of Vladien. Tell them I can go to the castle with you."

"Well?" the official demanded. "Is he who he says he is?"

"Yeah," Dracula huffed and turned on his heel, striding toward the castle.

Leith didn't wait for permission. He followed Dracula swiftly, hoping no one would stop him. Dracula looked straight ahead, ignoring Leith completely, as they moved away from the crowd, north to the castle.

The stone road dropped under the shadow sand, forcing them to walk slower. Dracula stopped at the base of the front stairs, looking up at the castle's main double doors. "Huh," he grunted.

"What?" Leith asked.

"There's something wrong here."

Leith looked up at the doors but couldn't detect what Dracula was talking about. He followed as Dracula slowly climbed the stairs. He stopped at the top, a suspicious glare in his eyes and beat his fist against the massive doors.

The hinges moaned as the doors swung inward. A single figure stood in the center of the entrance hall. Dracula gasped, alarming Leith, who was still too fuzzy brained to fully appreciate what he saw.

"What are you doing here, High Priest?" Dracula demanded, his arrogance faltering around the edges.

Rahaxeris looked past Dracula and fixed his ruby eyes on Leith. A smile stretched across his face, one so terrifying, Leith almost wet himself. He had no idea who this elf was, but it was plain he wanted his blood with a ravenous hunger.

Rahaxeris took a step forward. "You are behind the times, Dracula. Like always," he said calmly, not moving his gaze off Leith.

As the unknown predator stalked closer, Leith stood frozen in fear, even as his mind screamed *Run!*

Dracula's brow furrowed in confusion as he looked back at Leith and then to Rahaxeris. "He's not with me, High Priest," he declared loudly.

Rahaxeris reached out and seized Leith by the arm, his smile now obscenely wide. Caught in Rahaxeris' red gaze, like a bird hypnotized by the eyes of a snake, Leith made no struggle.

"Then I suggest you leave my presence before you share his fate," Rahaxeris said to Dracula.

Dracula took off into the castle as if his feet were on fire, no doubt looking for anyone who could explain what was going on.

Leith found himself towed along by his arm, his vision tunneling. Long empty hallways stretched out before him. Then he was maneuvered through a door into a dim, empty room and again faced with those terrible red eyes.

"Oh, you will never understand the restraint I'm exercising right now. How long I've waited, sat still and allowed you to live when doing so raged against everything inside me. You are going to suffer, Leith. You will know pain, and you will die."

Part of Leith's brain shook itself clear. He looked down at the hand on his forearm and then back into the stranger's face. "I don't know you. What have I done to deserve this?"

"What have you done? My dear boy, what haven't you done?"

Leith blinked a few times. "I'm very wealthy. If you are acting as a judge, listening to some accusers, I can make compensation. Amend my wrongs."

"I am not your judge, merely your custodian, and the only accuser around, is me."

Rahaxeris stood directly in front of Leith and grasped both of his shoulders. Leith began shaking violently with tears.

"Coward." Rahaxeris shook his head. "I'll not be the one to kill you, unless I am asked to. However, I desperately want to hurt you right now. Hmmm."

Rahaxeris slid his hands down Leith's arms stopping at his wrists. Leith screamed as Rahaxeris' long thumbnails cut open flesh.

"Look closely," Rahaxeris ordered.

Leith whimpered as he looked at the jagged open wounds on his wrists. Two black thorns appeared on top of the bloody mess. Leith screamed again, stumbling to his knees as Rahaxeris pushed the thorns into the wounds. He released Leith, who fell back, tearing at his wounds.

"It's already too late to dig them out."

"What are they?!" Leith cried.

"Memories. Past and future. Once the thorns reach your heart, you will lose all sense of yourself, at least for a while. You will live through the tortures you have created. You will feel the pain you have given to others. Not to mention the thorns themselves will cause excruciating pain with every beat of your heart."

"Take them out! Please! Please take them out!" he cried.

Rahaxeris smiled again as he turned to leave. "No. They have made me feel so much better, though I am far from satisfied. You should count yourself lucky. I'm capable of so much worse than this."

Rahaxeris shut the heavy door and locked it, holding the key. "Merhl!"

Merhl came quickly. "Yes, sir! How may I serve you?"

"Set a block on this door that no one can break except the one who has this key."

Rahaxeris handed Merhl the key so he could tie the power of the block with it. The block formed quickly and invisibly over the door. Merhl gave the key back.

"Thank you, Merhl. I need a large room for important company, one with a good view. Where could I find such a room?"

"Follow me, sir."

Leith's cries could still be heard faintly through the door.

Chapter Eight

Forest couldn't remember a time she felt so relaxed. Syrus kicked back on the couch, listening to music, while she called the closest pizza place that would deliver at four in the morning. When the middle-aged driver showed up a half hour later, she took pity on him and gave him a hundred dollar tip. Forest and Syrus plowed through the two large deep-dish pizzas like a pack of frat boys high on pot.

Now that her stomach wasn't tugging on her esophagus, Forest curled up against Syrus on the couch and let out a deep sigh of contentment.

"I was too distracted earlier to realize how hungry I was," Syrus said. "That was good. Almost as good as S'mores."

Forest chuckled. "I didn't realize you like S'mores *that* much. I think I have everything here to make them, well, except they won't be as good as they are when we have a fire."

"Let's wait then. We can have them at your cottage when we go back."

"Did you have enough? Are you full?"

He hesitated. "Yes and no."

"Oh? What else do you want?"

Syrus looked apologetic and shook his head. "Nothing. Never mind."

Forest swatted him on the shoulder. "Excuse me. You better tell me what it is you want, right now."

Syrus smirked. "I don't have to."

"Yes, you do. I'm your mate. I order you to spill it."

He leaned over and pressed his lips against hers. "I like hearing you say that,'" he said seriously.

"Say what?"

"Declare yourself my mate."

Forest wound her arms around his neck and nuzzled his ear. "Mate, lover, friend," she whispered.

"What would this be called here on earth?" he asked.

"Marriage."

"Marriage," Syrus tried the word out. "I like that. Is it very much the same?"

"No. It's a weaker bond than we share. People break their word to each other all the time. But with some people, marriage is lifelong and can be beautiful."

"So if we were married, I would be called your what?"

"Husband, and I would be your wife."

"Husband. I like that too."

Syrus kissed her again, and she could tell his mind had wandered back into the bedroom.

"Hang on. Let's begin on the right foot, with open, honest communication. Tell me what you wanted."

He gently took hold of her hand, brought her wrist up to his face, and inhaled deeply. "I want you. All there is of you. And I've yet to have the pleasure of your blood in my mouth."

"Oh," she said stupidly. *Duh.*

"I didn't want to ask because the last time I did, you rejected me. I didn't want to offend or disgust you."

Forest's eyes glazed momentarily as a nasty memory surfaced in her mind. Hazy, broken images of the time Leith drained her to the edge of death.

She stared openly at Syrus. His power was obvious from his magic down to his muscles. He could take anything he wanted by force. She'd seen him weaponize his rage in battle. He held all the power within him under perfect control.

Her eyes began to sting. One of the only vampire mages in existence, with all the potential to be a true monster, sat calmly next to her and gave her tenderness; offered her his heart.

She couldn't stop the tears that came as her heart clenched and ached with love for him. "Damn it," she said, wiping at the tears. "There you go again, making me weak."

Syrus looked alarmed. "I'm sorry. I'm sorry. I won't ever ask you again. I promise."

Forest laughed and pushed him down on the couch. She climbed on top of him, surprising him with her passion. "You're mine," she said fervently, crushing his mouth with hers. "Take everything you want."

And he did.

His bite was excruciatingly gentle. Forest had no idea it could be like this and it all but exploded her head with pleasure.

"I want to mark you," he whispered, barely taking his mouth from her skin. "I can't help it. It's my nature to mark my lover."

Forest rolled her eyes, sighing as she came crashing down from the clouds. "Way to kill my buzz, Syrus," she complained. "That was amazing, until you spoke."

"I'm sorry."

"Look, I thought this might come up and I understand it's your vampire instinct talking, but I'm not ready to have a new scar when I've only just rid myself of the others."

"I know, I know. I'm sorry. I get it."

"Maybe after my slave mark is gone, we can talk about it again...Maybe. It's just so unfair."

"Unfair?" Syrus asked.

"Yeah. You can mark me, but I can't mark you. It's unfair. The very idea makes me feel like property."

"I wish you could mark me. I want everyone to see it. I'd let you put your mark on my forehead."

Forest laughed.

"I'm serious. We should find some way you can mark me as your own."

"Hmm...we'll have to think about that. Now shut your mouth and put it to better use."

"Yes, ma'am."

****

Had it only been ten hours since she came home and found Syrus? Forest wondered as she closed her drapes, blocking out the harmful morning light. She considered the amount of time they'd spent sleeping and realized they had been together longer than that. This was the second dawn since they reunited. Syrus sat on the bed, his back against the headboard, lazily nibbling the edge of the last, cold pizza crust. Forest climbed back onto the bed and rested her head on his shoulder. "So what happened after I was banished?"

"I was placed in a prison, a portal with no destination. It was...terrible. The strength of the portal took my mage power from me." Syrus hung his head. "I'm so sorry, Forest. I failed you."

Forest laid her hand on his cheek. "Hey, don't say that. You didn't fail me. If anything, *I* failed you."

Syrus chuckled. "Preposterous."

"How did you get out?"

Syrus hesitated. "I'll tell you in a minute. What happened to you?"

"Your mother banished me. She wanted me dead, but she made it plain that she didn't want to get her hands dirty. Luckily, for me, the king ordered I was not to be harmed. But after I was shoved back here, I don't know what happened to his order, because the queen has been dropping assassins right through my ceiling."

Syrus took a ragged breath. "There's a lot I don't know. My father was called away in battle and unaware of what was happening to you…My mother is no longer a threat to you. She is now the one who is banished."

"The queen is banished? How? By whom?"

Syrus grimaced as the words came out. "Your father."

Dread stretched through her extremities. "My father," she whispered.

Syrus reached around her shoulders and pulled her close. "I don't know much, Forest. But he has taken over the Onyx Castle and banished my mother to another world. He broke me out of my prison, and he is the very thing you feared: a priest of the *Rune-dy*."

Forest's panic choked her. "He's coming for me. I always knew he would." She sat upright and grasped both of Syrus' shoulders. "You have to help me. I can't go back there! I have to stay where he can't get me!"

"Forest, we have to go back to Regia."

"No! I have to stay here!" she was speaking in hyper speed. "We can be happy here, Syrus. You'll see. I'll protect you from the sun. It'll be fine. More than fine."

Syrus pulled her tightly against his chest again. "Shh. It's all right. I don't think he means you any harm. If he did, why would he stop the threats against you? Why would he let me out and send me back here to be with you? I don't know what his plan is, but I don't think you need to fear him like this."

"But…what if he…"

"Think about it, Forest. If he can single handedly take over the Onyx Castle, do you really think you'd be safe from him here if he wanted to collect you?"

Forest tried to calm down and allow her reason to speak louder than her panic. "You met him?"

"Briefly."

"What is he like?"

"He's very powerful. His name is Rahaxeris."

Forest trembled. "Oh great. I know that name. I've heard it whispered with terror. He's the High Priest, *the leader*."

Strangely, Forest felt a shiver of joy through her fear. *I know my father's name.*

"It's going to be okay. I'll go back alone and see what's what. Then I'll come back for you."

Forest hesitated. "Okay. I guess that makes sense," she said slowly.

"We need more information."

Forest's mind raced. "I could go to the club and talk to whomever has taken over my old job. I'm sure they would know something."

Syrus shook his head. "The portals are closed."

"Why didn't you find out more before you came for me?"

Syrus chuckled and kissed her. "Desperation, my love. I barely absorbed the little information I received as it was." He kissed her again more deeply. "I could think of nothing but you."

"So how are you going to get back, if the portals are shut?" she asked.

"With this." Syrus pulled a silvery chain from the pocket of his trousers.

The light from the bedside lamp slipped along the alien metal, unable to grasp it. Forest took the chain from Syrus and examined the little ball hanging from it. "What is it?"

"An End of the Bridge. The ogre, who opened the portal here, gave it to me. Once I break it, it will take me back."

A solid weight clung to each of Forest's vertebrae as she watched Syrus get dressed and ready to leave. He seemed calm and collected. She felt a faceless distress, and her thoughts were ambushed in countless *what ifs*. What if the whole thing was a trap? What if the End of the Bridge didn't work properly and took Syrus to the wrong place where he would be in danger? What if her father killed Syrus when he saw that he returned without her?

Syrus kissed her lightly. "Okay, I'll be right back for you. It shouldn't take me any longer than a day."

"Okay." *No! Not okay.*

Syrus broke the ball between his hands and a black portal opened in the middle of her living room. He walked into it. One single second encapsulated all of the pain of separation she'd suffered over the last months.

"No!" Forest screamed and ran into the closing portal.

Syrus was ahead of her in the rushing darkness. She reached out and grabbed hold of him.

"What are you doing?" he shouted over the noise of the wind.

"We can't be apart again!"

The portal dumped them in a bare, empty room of the Onyx Castle. They both stood perfectly still for a moment, listening and waiting. Nothing happened.

"I thought we'd be in the throne room," Forest whispered.

"So did I. Not that I'm complaining. I can do without the fanfare." He rubbed his hands on her trembling shoulders. "It's going to be okay. No matter what, I won't let you go."

The creaking of the door's hinges had Syrus stepping protectively in front of Forest. She peeked over his shoulder to see a small vampire maid curtsy to them.

"Sir, madam, please follow me."

Forest's mind tripped. *What the fraz?*

Syrus shrugged and pulled her along by the hand. The hall was completely empty. They followed the swift-walking maid, who led them through a few long passages and up two stories.

"Your room," the maid said, stopping and gesturing to a large, ornate door. "If there is anything else you desire just ring the bell." She bobbed another curtsy and walked away.

"Well, I see they've prepared for our arrival." Syrus chuckled. "It's a little odd to be shown to a guest room in your own house. I guess that means it's not mine anymore."

"Of course it is!" Forest said forcefully. "You're the future king."

He kissed her lightly. "Maybe I am. Maybe I'm not. Come on."

Syrus opened the door and walked into the room, leaving Forest standing on the threshold.

"It's not booby-trapped." His smile was teasing.

Forest came slowly into the vast room, trying to not be impressed at the luxury. Never had she felt so misplaced. The view from the window drew her magnetically, and she drifted toward it when something in the corner caught her eye.

"Oh!" Forest ran to her locker. "Thank you, Syrus!"

"For what?"

"For getting my locker from Fortress." She caressed the carved wooden doors, unlocking them with her touch.

"Forest, I didn't. I didn't do any of this."

"Then who? Kindel must have done it." The doors swung open. Happy tears rose behind her eyes as she spotted her sword. Snatching it up, she held it to her breast, running her fingers along the hilt. "Oh, Syrus, my sword is here! I thought I'd never see it again."

Syrus came up behind her and placed his hands lovingly on her shoulders. "I'm glad you're happy."

Having her sword back momentarily eclipsed everything else, but her questions and nerves resurfaced quickly. She laid it down and closed the locker.

A sharp knock vibrated the door.

"Syrus?!" the voice on the other side was rife with desperation.

Syrus moved toward the door. "Dad?" He lifted the latch.

King Zeren charged through the door and engulfed Syrus in a rib-breaking hug. "Oh, my son! You're safe! I'm so glad to see you!" Zeren released him reluctantly and looked at him thoroughly. "Your sight?"

"No, Father. I will always be blind."

"You must tell me everything."

"I will. And I'll start with the most important. Father, this is Forest."

Zeren fixed his eyes on Forest. Her heart leapt into her throat. She wasn't prepared for formal introductions. She had no idea what her face, hair, or body looked like, and she was wearing plaid boxer shorts and a faded T-shirt. Groaning internally, she straightened her spine and lifted her chin. She would apologize for nothing. If she had a call to be nervous, then so did Zeren. The glare of inspection he used on her, she served right back to him. Zeren noticed. He raised one imperious eyebrow for a moment before smiling at her as though she were the cutest thing he'd ever seen.

Syrus got his looks from his father, Forest noted. Zeren had the same grey in his eyes and the same bone structure to his face. His long braided hair was greying at the top, and his skin was wrinkled with age and decades of worry.

Zeren walked up to her. "Forest, it is an honor to meet you." He took her hand and kissed it. "I look forward to getting to know you. There is so much going on right now. Regia is in such upheaval, but never fear, we shall have a grand party to celebrate your connection, very soon."

"Oh..." *Damn, a party. Crap.* "There's no need to..."

"I know there is nothing I can really do to apologize for Christiana's behavior. I swear I did not know about it. I am your servant." He gave a little bow. "If there is anything you desire, if it is within my power, you shall have it."

"Uh, thank you."

"Oh, here. I was supposed to give you this." Zeren pulled a sealed letter from his cloak and handed it to her.

She knew who must have sent it. Everything around her seemed to fade into shadow. Zeren and Syrus talked, but the words turned into an incomprehensible murmuring in her ears. She stared at her name written on the paper. When she finally looked up again, Zeren was gone and Syrus sat quietly on a chair by the bed. Hesitation took its time. There was knowledge in this letter. Did she want the knowledge? Did she need it? Or the man who offered it? He had always known who she was, where she was, and this was the first letter her father had bothered to write. The temptation to burn it or throw it out the window, unread, pushed into her hands.

The temptation proved hollow.

Forest opened it with shaking hands. She didn't know if she was ready for this but it was happening. Her eyes fell hungrily on her father's handwriting.

Forest,

You cannot know how happy it makes me to have you reading this. I apologize if this letter comes off wrong. I do not often suffer from indecision, but the words I should use here elude me. I am anxious for our first discussion and will be waiting for you in a protected and private place. Take your time and when you are ready, ring for the maid, and she will lead you to me.

Your father,

Rahaxeris

Forest took a deep breath. What had she expected? It said nothing really. She read it over twice then read it aloud to Syrus.

"So what do you think?" she asked.

"Seems pretty straight forward to me. He just wants to talk to you."

Forest wanted to ask Syrus to come with her, but pride stopped her. That would look weak. She analyzed her thoughts, amazed to discover the natural desire of a child to please the parent was inside her. Through all of the emotions she had ever had regarding her father—hate, anger, disappointment, indignation, and heartbreak—

she still wanted his approval, and she innately knew weakness would displease him.

Why the hell do I care? She couldn't answer her own question.

Well, she knew one thing for sure. She wasn't going to meet her father in her pajamas. She opened the closet and groaned. Nothing but dresses and elegant gowns. Tiny healed slippers, embroidered with designs and shiny beads, winked in the light along the floor. What the devil were those good for except breaking your ankles?

As she ventured deeper into the uber-feminine space, she found drawers of stockings, and corsets, and jewelry. A word she had not yet formulated in her mind since completing her connection with Syrus swam sickeningly into her awareness. *Princess.* She grabbed the skirt of the nearest hanging gown and rubbed the fabric between her thumb and forefinger. She envisioned the grand party Zeren promised they'd have and countless other official functions and dinners she'd be expected to attend. Her heart sank, and the urge to run away overtook her. Fate had made a terrible mistake. She should never have been paired with Syrus.

Forest took a deep breath, scrubbing her hands over her face. These clothes might be her size but they would never really fit. She would be ridiculous to everyone who witnessed her attempt, and worse, she would make a laughingstock of Syrus. The idea of anyone laughing at Syrus put a fire in her belly and she instantly snapped out of her self-pity.

What was she thinking? She used to be a Fortress operative. Playing a part was easy for her. More than anything, she just wanted to be herself, but she could do the public stuff…for Syrus. Parties and functions aside, no way was she going to meet her father dressed like a Disney character. She pushed further back into the closet and discovered a small treasure. Three basic, unassuming drawers, filled with clothes she could actually use. Shirts, socks, pants, all made of Regian fabric, but there in the very bottom, four neatly folded pairs of jeans and a stiff new pair of combat boots! *Yes!*

Forest bathed quickly, hardly noticing the elegance of the private bathroom. Wrapped in a towel, she wiped the steam off the mirror and considered how to arrange her appearance. She shifted through a few faces, but nothing seemed right. Forest looked at her true face for a moment. Physically incapable of showing her true face to anyone but Syrus, she decided to mimic it as closely as she could.

She ran her hands through the length of her hair, enjoying its natural appearance. She altered the color of her warm chestnut curls to a slightly metallic bronze. When she finished creating her look, she could have been mistaken for her own sister. Bracing her hands on the sink, she looked directly into her own eyes in the mirror. *I know who I am. I'm ready.*

Chapter Nine

Forest stared at the wood grain on the door, wiping her sweaty palms on her jeans. The servant had vanished as soon as she showed Forest where her father was waiting, leaving her utterly alone. Did he know she was there, just on the other side of the door? Could he hear her heart thrashing? Smell her fear?

The thought appalled her. She shook herself and squared her shoulders. The door swung open a little faster than she had intended and banged loudly against the wall. She submerged a grimace and kept her face blank.

Rahaxeris rose fluidly from his chair, his red eyes fastened tightly on her. She visibly absorbed everything about his appearance. His hair hung straight to his shoulders, and the light glimmered on the golden shafts. His face was narrow and harsh like a manga character. His hands were long and sharp as if they could slice through skin just by touching. His eyes were the same shape as hers. Aside from that, she didn't see any other physical resemblance to her true form. He had an odd kind of beauty, but beauty nonetheless.

Father. Her mind tested the word carefully. No rejection or denial arose inside her.

She licked her lips. "Father?"

"Yes, I am."

Silence. Just a moment, necessary after verbal confirmation. Rahaxeris sat back down and gestured to the empty chair opposite his. Forest closed the door and sat down. She stared openly at him. He was terrifying, yet she was not afraid. He waited passively for her to speak. A whole minute passed.

"I know you have questions, Forest. I swear I'll answer anything you ask honestly and unedited."

Forest took a deep breath. *All right. Here goes.* "Why? Why now? You could have contacted me at any time. Why now?"

"It's the first time I have been at liberty to contact you. If I could have been a part of your life before now, I would have."

"I don't understand," Forest said slowly.

"I think we should begin at the beginning, don't you?"

Forest hesitated, feeling as though she were standing on the edge of cliff. She could go on without this knowledge. Did she really need it? Did she even want it?

"I'm listening." Her voice was barely more than a whisper.

Rahaxeris nodded his head approvingly and began. "I haven't always been the High Priest of the *Rune-dy*. Before you were born, I worked in the science department. I began a proposal for a long-term experiment that I presented to my fellow priests. They all agreed, and everyone was involved on some level."

"I don't care about how you rose to power. I want to know if you loved my mother, and why you abandoned me," Forest cut in.

"I'll get to it. May I continue?"

Forest crossed her arms over her chest. He plunged ahead.

"The experiment was my idea, so I was the foreman. My fellow priests followed my instructions with the exception of Menjel, the High Priest at that time. He was mildly interested in the project. However, it's important that you know I only had limited control."

"So what was this all-important experiment?" Forest demanded impatiently.

Rahaxeris took a slow, shaky breath. "Splicing."

Run. Plug your ears. Leave. Leave now!

Forest's mouth fell open, and she turned her eyes to the floor.

"The experiment was designed to discover what, if any, combinations of our races would create a superior being. Women and men of every race were screened for the trial…there was no sex. Every child was created in the lab…except one.

"I never intended using my own DNA in the process, but when I met Liasia… I had a premonition. She was so strong, had such a fire in her spirit. I reviewed every male donor and found I couldn't stomach the idea of watering down her fire with lesser material. I knew, instinctively, it had to be me. It could have been there, cold and sterile in the lab, but she attracted me. We became lovers."

Forest closed her eyes, placing her head in her hands.

"Forest?"

"I'm nothing more than an experiment? Created for the sole purpose of data collection?"

"Yes."

She stood up abruptly, her chair skittering across the floor behind her. "You have no heart!" she shouted. "Why couldn't you have lied to me? I always believed it was nothing more than shame on your part. I was the product of a secret affair you had to hide to reach your political ambitions. That would have been so much better. I thought you knew nothing about my life, but I was wrong. You have notes! Pages! *Files!* Don't you?!"

Rahaxeris pointed a long sharp finger at the chair behind her. The chair slid across the floor, back to its original position. "Please sit back down. There is more I need to tell you."

Forest turned and brought her foot down on the seat, splintering the wood. His expression remained stoic as he pointed at the broken chair, repairing it instantly. Forest's eyebrows shot up as she regarded the chair, shocked momentarily out of her pain. "Will I ever be able to do that?"

A smile broke across his face. "Perhaps. Please sit back down."

Forest sat, building walls quickly around her heart, and looked at the floor again. "What happened to the other hybrid children?"

"Destroyed. Most deemed *unsuccessful*."

Forest cringed away from him.

"Yes. You're right, Forest. I'm a monster."

"Why was I allowed to live?" she asked.

"My instincts told me you would be a successful product. The whole experiment provided no surprises, except one…I never anticipated I would love my child."

Forest lifted her eyes.

"Your mother told you, I named you, on the day you were born?"

"Yes."

"And that I never saw you again?"

Forest nodded.

"That was a lie. I saw you. Many times. I rocked you to sleep every night until you were two. But I had to cease all contact. It was becoming dangerous for me. My position in the *Rune-dy* was shaky. I couldn't let the others know how I felt about you. They questioned my decision to father you myself as it was. Menjel called for your destruction. I convinced my fellow priests to allow you to live so we could see how your gifts might mature as you became an adult. They all agreed so long as there was no interference in your life. Simply observe and nothing more."

Forest grated her teeth together, pushing back tears. "You know everything about me, don't you?"

"I know the events of your life, but I don't know how you feel or what you think. I want to."

"Then you must know about Leith." Humiliation slammed down on her.

Rahaxeris stood up abruptly and strode to the window. His shoulders shook as he braced the frame with his hands. "I'm so sorry, Forest. I thought I was doing the right thing by sending you to the Academy. Once I saw the mistake, it was too late for me to undo it. I'd fought so hard against the other priests to get you in there...After...after you caught Leith's attention, Menjel morbidly wanted to know what the outcome would be. It was then I knew I had to do something. I began planning to take over the *Rune-dy.*

"I've done unspeakable things, Forest. Things I hope you never learn about. But I achieved my goal of becoming High Priest."

"Wow," Forest said acidly, "that's terrific. I'm gratified you could do the things you set out to do, all the while leaving me a slave."

"Maybe I chose the wrong path. But I'm here now to fix things. I had to become High Priest to make a better world *for you.* That's the only reason I've done all this."

"*Fix things!*" Forest spat. "How are you going to fix things?"

Rahaxeris turned to face her. "I am the High Priest of the *Rune-dy.* I have more power than any person or government in Regia. *And you're my daughter.* And now the world will know it." He strode back to his chair and sat down. "I have two gifts for you," he said, pulling the green stone necklace and the key from his robes. He reached out and placed both in her palm.

"I've done fine on my own. I don't think I want people to know I'm the monster's daughter. I'll figure things out on my own." Forest lifted her hand to throw the necklace and key but he was too fast for her. Rahaxeris caught her hand and gently folded her fingers over the gifts.

"I understand. But please just hold on to these for a while and think about what I'm offering you."

Forest looked down at her clasped hand and curiosity got the better of her. "Just what are you offering me, exactly?"

"This is your birthright." He pulled the necklace out of her grasp and held it up. "A title, created uniquely for you. All you have to do is accept it. I know of your political ambitions; now you can surpass even your wildest dreams. If you accept, you will be *Hailemarris.* Supreme judge."

It was as though he were speaking a foreign language. Her mind couldn't process his words. There was just too much happening to her too fast. She moved past it, deciding she could think about it all alone, later.

"And this key?"

"That key opens the door to your captive enemy. You may dispatch him any time you wish, or I will happily do the honors if you don't want to."

A lump rose in Forest's throat. "Leith? Leith is here? In the castle?"

"Yes. And you might consider keeping the information to yourself until you're prepared to kill him, otherwise your mate might tear the castle down stone by stone, trying to get him first."

Forest stared at her hand, shaking. Her lungs refusing to fill completely when she breathed.

"It's all right," he said gently. "Take your time. Consider what you want to do. I will support you no matter what you decide. And if you want to talk to me again, I'll be here."

He walked to the door and opened it, hesitating before turning back to her. "Remember, monster that I am, I love you. I have from the very first, and nothing matters to me as much as you do."

The door closed behind him, leaving her alone.

Forest walked slowly back to her room in a daze, the key and necklace clasped tightly in her hand. A void inside swallowed everything, leaving her lost and confused. Her emotional nerve endings had stretched too thin and gone comatose in defense. What was she going to do now?

Syrus greeted her when she opened the door but there was nothing but ringing in her ears. Unaware of what he said, she shoved the necklace at him. "Please keep this safe for me."

He followed her to her locker, muttering unintelligible words, while she strapped her sword around her waist. She had to side step him as she went into the closet. Heading straight for the jewelry, Forest grabbed the first necklace she saw with a sturdy looking chain. She removed and tossed the jewel aside, then strung the key on it and fastened it around her neck.

Syrus was still talking to her, waving his hands agitatedly.

"I'm sorry," she said carefully, unable to hear her own voice over the ringing. "I have to go now. I'll be back soon. Don't worry. Don't follow."

She ran from the room into the hall, the ringing fading away. Turning down a corridor, she almost collided with someone blocking her way.

Rahaxeris stood dead center, preventing her from passing. Merhl stood demurely behind him, his eyes turned to the ground.

"Where are you going, Forest?"

"What do you care?! Am I a prisoner now?"

"Hardly." Rahaxeris held out a silvery, End of the Bridge to her. "Tell Merhl where you want to go."

Forest hesitated, not wanting anyone to know where she was going, but the urgent desire to get there superseded. She snatched the End of the Bridge and pocketed it.

"I want to go to the Wolf's Wood."

Rahaxeris stepped to the side as Merhl gave her a little bow and then struck the air. A black portal opened, and Forest ran into it without a backward glance.

Chapter Ten

"Shi!" Forest yelled to the trees, her voice racked with despair.

The portal dumped her a half mile from the Heart. The stinging pull of the Heart's power reached deep inside, shattering her defenses, breaking the walls. She immediately began moving away from it. Running, tears streaming down her cheeks, searching for her surrogate mother.

"Shi!"

A soft wind circled around her. She stopped running. The breeze caressed and soothed, softening the sharp edges of the storm within her. Shi embraced her with the whirlwind before appearing in her corporeal form. "What is it, daughter?" she asked.

Forest wanted to collapse into Shi's arms but of course, she couldn't. Instead, she crumpled to the ground at her feet, unable to articulate the foul truth of who and what she really was. And mercifully she didn't have to; Shi could see everything inside her.

Shi knelt next to her and placed her ghostly hand on the back of Forest's head. "It doesn't matter, Forest. You should have stayed and talked to Syrus."

"I couldn't tell him," Forest cried. "It's not fair to him. None of this is. He shouldn't be with me. He deserves better. A princess."

"He's had one."

Forest's head snapped up. "What?"

Shi smiled. "You two don't know each other very well yet. You're little better than strangers. It's really for him to tell you, but I won't string you along. Syrus was engaged to a noble's daughter before he lost his sight."

Forest's eyes, previously blurred with tears, now blurred with red.

Shi chuckled. "Ah, I see you don't like that. You're jealous and possessive. You should pay attention to that. Don't doubt your love for him."

"It doesn't matter what *I* feel. He shouldn't be with me. Now more than ever. I'm just an…" The word rose in her throat like vomit. "…experiment."

"And a slave?" Shi prompted.

"Yes. A slave."

Shi touched the chain around Forest's neck. "A slave with the power to free herself. I don't understand why you came to see me before killing Leith."

"I don't know. I can't understand what I'm thinking. Have I lost my senses?"

Shi hesitated as she listened carefully to the tempest of Forest's heart, concern growing stronger by the second. "I'm glad you came to me first."

"What happened to 'you should have stayed and talked to Syrus'?"

"You *do* need to talk to Syrus. But you need to calm down. You've just suffered a terrible blow, and it has knocked you momentarily stupid. Take the knowledge of your father and your origin like medicine. Don't gag on it. Just take it all in and relax."

Shi felt like a traitor, but she took the only action she could think of; she put Forest into a deep sleep then moved her to a soft, leafy place and caused the flowers to bloom all around her. Not since Forest was a child had Shi felt such reckless self-destruction within her. She reached in and stroked out every good memory she could find in Forest's sub-conscious, creating a quilted dream of peace, happiness, and feelings of love. She wove the depth of her own love for Forest into the dream, begging it to imbue her with the concrete knowledge that she was worthwhile, that she was loved.

Chapter Eleven

Confusion and rage vibrated through Syrus. He felt too much. His heart pulled in too many directions. Forest had left him without a word as to where she was going. She gave him a weird amulet and told him to take care of it! What in the hell was that about? He could feel she was in no physical danger, but oh! The heartbreak she was suffering! He had to know what was going on. Why did his love feel such black emotions?

The pulsing red sphere of rage began to solidify in his chest. *Not yet.* He pushed it down. First, he would find the blackguard who claimed to be her father, give him the shakedown of his life, and then decide about kicking his unnatural ass.

Syrus rang the infernal bell and waited for a servant to arrive. The door had barely creaked open when Syrus barked to the person behind it the order that he wanted to see Redge immediately. He needed his wingman.

"Come in!" Syrus bellowed when a knock came to the door.

Redge entered the room. Syrus embraced him roughly, instantly feeling steadier with his best friend back with him. "Man, it's good to see you, Redge."

"You too, my lord. You've got to catch me up. There's madness going round this place." Redge was usually more reserved.

"I will. You need to catch me up, too. There's just too damn much going on. My father gave me the gist of what was happening in the war but not the details, and I'm dying to know all about it, but now I've got a personal crisis on my hands. I need your help."

"Whatever I can do. Is Forest all right?"

"What do you know?!" Syrus demanded grabbing Redge by the front of his shirt.

"What? What do I know about what?!"

"Forest! Where is she?!"

Redge tried to ease Syrus back. "I'll tell you everything I know. It will be easier if you let go."

Syrus checked himself. He hadn't meant to grab Redge. "I'm sorry." He stepped back. "She's got me going crazy."

Redge straightened his shirt, the hint of a smile on his mouth. "I see that. Maybe we should sit down. You're going to need to practice your self-control while I talk."

Syrus had never put so much of his mage power into holding himself still as he did while Redge told him about all that happened after he was imprisoned by Christiana.

"I swear to you, I did my best to protect Forest from the queen. And I searched for you day and night, knowing you were still in the castle, trapped. I finally got one of the ogres to talk, but then Christiana began sending assassins to kill Forest. I intercepted a few. She caught wind of what I was doing, and she sent me to the front lines. Her minions ambushed me in the hall and threw me into a portal before I could blink an eye. I guess I'm lucky she didn't kill me."

Syrus took a deep breath. "I'm glad you're okay. You did your best for Forest. I appreciate it."

"I'm surprised she survived such an onslaught."

"Oh, she can take care of herself," Syrus said with pride. "Petite little kickass…I love her so much."

Redge smirked. He could never consider Syrus weak or pathetic, but man was he whipped. Redge was amazed as Syrus told him all about his journey to Maxcarion and everything that happened with Forest. Equally, Syrus was amazed to learn that Philippe was dead and the war was practically over before it began.

"So now, this *Rune-dy* shows up, takes over, and Zeren hardly bats an eye." Redge shook his head. "Oh, and Dracula is back."

"Oh?"

"Yeah. Just this morning, and now he's whispering some insanity that the *Rune-dy* ambushed him as soon as he crossed the castle's threshold but let him go because he got Leith instead."

Syrus jumped to his feet. "Leith?!"

"That's what Dracula said. Said the High Priest wanted his blood and that Leith is more than likely dead or in the grips of torture right now." Redge's eyebrows shot up. He'd never seen Syrus look so bloodthirsty. "Obviously, this means something to you."

"Come on!" Syrus ran out the door.

Redge followed on Syrus' heels as he rushed through the halls, shoving aside anyone who got in his way.

"RAHAXERIS!" Syrus bellowed. "RAHAXERIS! ANSWER ME!"

There was no answer. They continued to run down to the ground floor of the castle. Syrus burst through the doors into the throne room. It was empty except for security. He stopped in the center of the room, a tornado holding still.

Redge spotted Merhl standing against the wall. "Let me see what I can find out," he said to Syrus before turning to the ogre. "Merhl?"

The ogre brought his eyes up from the floor.

"Is Rahaxeris still in the castle?"

Merhl turned his eyes back to the ground. "I am unsure, sir."

Redge crossed his arms over his chest, recognizing the lie. "I understand everything has changed in the castle. It's confusing for all of us, Merhl. But you are still subject to the crown, are you not?"

Merhl hesitated, shifting his feet. "I don't know, sir. I think so."

"Prince Syrus needs your help. He needs to speak to Rahaxeris. It's urgent. He must learn the fate of his kinsman, Leith."

Merhl's eyes darted up for a second then settled back to the floor.

"He's in the castle, isn't he?"

"Vladien's son is being held in the castle under arrest. No one can open the door to his cell except the one who has the key."

"Wanna bet? Show us the way," Syrus ordered.

Merhl's eyes lifted to Syrus, unmistakable fear clouding them. Twisting his deformed hands, he bowed. "Yes, Your Highness."

Syrus and Redge followed Merhl through the dark, winding halls until he stopped in front of a plain wooden door. Syrus ran his hand over the energy. "Break it," he ordered Merhl.

"I cannot. I was given orders."

"*I'm* giving you orders!"

"Rahaxeris' word supersedes yours. I'm sorry. I cannot break it."

Red lightening cracked and snaked over Syrus' arms. Redge stepped back in fear.

"You break it open or I'll break you!" Syrus roared.

"ENOUGH, SYRUS!" Rahaxeris strode toward them, radiating waves of calm energy and stepping protectively in front of Merhl. "Calm yourself."

"I'll be calm when Leith's blood covers my skin."

"That's not going to happen."

"Do you know who and what that is behind that door?" Syrus demanded.

"Of course. I'm the one who put him there."

"I'm Forest's mate. It's my right to kill him, and I'm not moving until I've exercised that right."

"*I'm* Forest father. I could claim the same right, and I understand more than anyone else how badly you want to dispatch him. But I will not and neither shall you. His fate rests with Forest. She will not be denied the pleasure of vanquishing her enemy. Not even by you, unless she asks you to do the wet work for her. Until then, you shall endure."

Syrus' fists were clenched and shaking, but the lightening re-absorbed under his skin.

Rahaxeris smiled. "Don't worry. I don't think she'll let him live much longer."

Syrus took three deep breaths. "All right. You're right. It should be her." Unable to stand Rahaxeris' society a moment longer, he turned on his heel and walked away. Redge followed. At the end of the hall, Syrus stopped and turned back. "I won't let you hurt her. And if you do…"

Rahaxeris smiled again. "Likewise."

Syrus stormed back into the empty throne room and began pacing its length. Every few steps a snap of red electricity sparked along his hands.

"Hey, man, you look like you could use some time away," Redge suggested.

"Yes. But I'm not leaving until Forest returns."

"Well, you need to blow off some steam at least. Wanna go to the armory and spar?"

Syrus stopped pacing. "Yeah. Definitely."

They headed out of the throne room, down to the bowels of the castle.

"Just please don't kick my ass too hard," Redge pleaded.

Chapter Twelve

Forest awoke slowly, a peaceful internal feeling pulsing through her. She blinked and looked around. Evening had come to the Wood, and the faint glow of Shi shimmered next to her.

"How are you feeling?"

"How am I feeling?" The sweet peace inside her snapped, replaced by anger. "You put me to sleep?"

"Sorry. I had to. Your mind was clouded with madness."

Forest rubbed her eyes, reality resurfacing from her sleepy brain. "Damn."

Shi moved closer and wrapped her whisper of an arm around Forest's shoulders. "You must overcome."

Tears pushed through Forest's eyes. "I don't know if I can."

"If only you could see yourself through my eyes. Through Syrus' eyes, and yes, even though Leith's."

"Leith's?"

"Think about who he is. Why would he have enslaved you?"

"Because he hates me." Forest shrugged.

"Oh, yes. He hates you, but not because you're a Halfling. He hates you because he's jealous of you." Shi laid her hand over Forest's heart. "He wants to possess the fire that burns here. You are everything he is not and can never be."

Forest shook her head and looked down. "I'm nothing. An experiment. Cells and tissue created for the purpose of data collection."

"You always believed you were just a bastard. Why is this so much worse?" Shi demanded angrily.

Forest lifted her hands up in front of her face, her whole body shaking. "Look! Look how disgusting I am! Creature. Monster. *Thing*." She leaned over and vomited.

Forest lay back down, curled into the fetal position.

"Unique. Gifted. Original. Beautiful warrior with a fire soul. *That* is what you are, Forest! And now you are a princess, too."

"Damn it!" Forest shouted, springing to her feet. "That too! Stacked on top of it all, I have to be mated to Syrus. And as soon as the world knows about us, I can offer him nothing but shame…And I won't do it. I tell you, I won't!"

Shi blinked at her mildly. "Maybe you should sleep a bit longer."

Forest growled, unable to articulate a retort.

"Syrus loves you."

"Yes, he does," Forest said aggressively. "And that will blind him to the inevitable."

"Do you not return his love at all?"

"Why do you think I can't stand the idea of humiliating him?" Forest paced, wringing her hands. "Our bond has to be broken. And I think I've figured out how."

"You cannot go through with it, Forest," Shi said sternly. "This insane idea that leaving Leith alive is your out with Syrus."

"Sometimes I hate how you can read my thoughts." Unconsciously Forest ran her fingers across her scar. "This scar stands in the way of me and Syrus truly being together…So maybe if…perhaps…"

"Are you not at all afraid of the pain of rejecting your life mate? I know you've heard the stories."

Forest shrugged.

"Leith must die!" Shi demanded.

"Why? Why must he? His life is in my hands. I can do what I want with it."

"Everything you're contemplating will only break you in the process. Syrus too."

Forest shook her head, not listening. "I can do this. I can figure this out."

"The only thing you need to figure out is who you really are," Shi said acidly. "You have always wanted to have an influence, it's what you've worked so hard for, for so many years. Now you have the chance to have more influence than you've ever dreamed, and you run from it... You have great ability to do good."

"I have to go back."

"Wait, Forest! You need more time. You're not ready!"

Forest ignored her and smashed the End of the Bridge between her hands.

Forest landed in the throne room. The fading light of the sunset streamed through the windows, washing the stone floor in rich colors. She looked up at the two thrones, a sinking feeling weighing down her stomach. It wasn't her fantasy. Influence, Shi had said. She *did* want influence, not absolute power.

Two male courtiers came into the room. They looked around the room furtively then seemed to relax. Forest was reminded of fops she'd seen in movies. One of them spotted her and elbowed his companion nodding in her direction. Forest remained still as they sauntered up to her. One sneering, one leering.

The leering one grabbed her hand and raised it to his lips. "Good evening, Lady. And just who might you be?"

Forest tucked her fingers inside his and pulled his hand toward her, inspecting it. "Ugh. Look at your hands. You call yourself a man? Your hands are more feminine than mine." She tossed his hand back at him.

His smile faltered for a second before stretching across his face again. "I'd like to see you say that after you experience what I can do with them."

Forest snorted derisively.

The sneering one grabbed a handful of her hair and sniffed. "She's a new addition to the harem, perhaps? Since when do we have elves in the harem?"

"Maybe since that *Rune-dy* took over. I'll have to thank him." He reached for her hand again. "Come with me to my room."

"You've made a little mistake. Now back off before it becomes a grave mistake."

The sneering one grabbed her arm roughly. "Big words, little girl. Apparently you don't know who you're dealing with."

Forest blinked at him then threw her head back laughing.

"How dare y—"

Forest grabbed the hand on her arm and pried his wimpy fingers loose easily. Locking her hands over his, she jumped into the air, tucked into a full flip, pulled him off his feet and broke his wrist. His scream echoed around the room.

He crumpled to the floor, holding his hand and whimpering. The admiring one put his hands up in surrender and backed away. "Who *are* you?" he asked.

"Forest," she said aggressively over her shoulder as she left the room.

"Can you believe what she did?" the crying one on the floor asked his friend.

He placed his hand over his heart, looking down at the other. "I think I'm in love."

Forest kept her head down, looking at no one as she walked through the halls back to her room. Her curiosity over where Leith was being held and what he was enduring was diminished by her need to see Syrus. But the key hanging around her neck now felt like a lead weight.

Syrus wasn't in their room. She took a deep breath and closed her eyes, focusing on him. He was close by, somewhere in the castle. Did he know Leith was here? What could she possibly say to him? What exactly was her plan? How could she avoid hurting him?

She looked down at her attire and decided to dress for bed. She dragged her feet to the closet. Her arms were heavy as she dug through the drawers, yawning deeply. Trimmed in lace and ribbons, nothing looked comfortable. How was anyone supposed to sleep in such things?

Defeated by the selection, she pulled a silky white nightgown over her head and stalked to the bed.

****

She hadn't meant to fall asleep. But the sky was completely dark outside the window when Forest opened her eyes. Her solitude now felt very empty and cold.

Footsteps coming swiftly up the hall sounded through the door. She sat up as Syrus charged in, covered in sweat and a delighted beam on his face. That innocent smile slew her from across the room. She melted. "You're back!" Forest climbed out of the bed.

He rushed toward her then stopped abruptly. "I'm all yucky."

"I don't care."

"No, no. Let me get clean...You smell like heaven. I'll be right back. Don't move."

She followed him to the bathroom and leaned on the doorframe. "What have you been doing?"

Syrus chuckled as he pulled his drenched shirt over his head. "I've been sparring with Redge and a few well trained ogres. Man, I've missed fighting, being stuck in that accursed portal for months." His smile vanished abruptly as he turned the water on. "We need to talk…once I'm clean. It's important so don't fall asleep while I'm bathing."

"All right," Forest said lamely as she closed the door.

She paced the room, her thoughts jumbled, her heart thumping erratically. Syrus came out a few minutes later wrapped in a silky black robe. Forest blew out a breath. Damn, he was gorgeous; it wasn't fair. Too bad he was all serious and wanted to talk.

He enveloped her in his arms and she pressed her lips against his bare chest. He stroked her hair back from her face and kissed her temple. "You're distracting me, and I need to talk to you," he chuckled.

"Go get dressed then or acquiesce to my hormones."

He pulled away reluctantly and disappeared into the closet. Forest sighed and sat down on the bed. He came back out wearing loose trousers and a plain tunic and sat down on the bed next to her. "This life mate thing is a killer."

His statement caught her off guard. "What?"

He put his hand over his heart. "All day, I could feel your pain but didn't know what caused it. Is it the same for you?"

"Oh, yes. I can feel what you're feeling, but I can't hear your thoughts. Although, I'm not sure I felt anything from you today…I guess I was a little self-absorbed. Sorry. Was there something you wanted me to feel?"

"No. I want to know what happened with your father."

Forest shivered. "Oh, Syrus…I'm so tired… and it's so awful." She took a deep breath, seeing no way of escape. "He told me about when…when I was conceived." Tears swelled again as the words came pouring out of her.

Syrus' face remained impassive, and she hated herself more with every word she spoke. Her sprit sank so low it seemed to fuse with the floor. She told him about the necklace and the title that was offered to her. She told him everything except that Rahaxeris had given Leith to her as a gift.

When Forest stopped talking, waiting for Syrus to speak, all he did was cross his arms over his chest and frown a little. "Where did you run off to?" he asked.

"To the Wood. To see Shi."

"Ah. Yes, I should have thought of that. I was so worried."

"I'm sorry. I should have stayed. I was overwhelmed." Forest's shoulders dropped downward, and she hung her head.

"Is that all?"

"Yes," she lied.

"There's something else you need to know. Leith is in the castle, under arrest. I want to take you there so you can kill him. Rahaxeris said you are the only one who can open the door." He grabbed her hand. "Just think baby. Your freedom, here and now."

"Not now. Not yet."

"What do you mean?"

"I…I'm too tired."

Syrus stood up. "Forest, what the hell?"

Sobs rose in her throat. "Don't yell at me! I can't take it right now."

"Okay, so you're too tired. Maybe you've been through too much today to understand what I've just told you."

"I understand. I just want to…to make a ritual of it when I kill him. Not when I'm exhausted and in my nightgown."

Syrus' ire fizzled. He sighed. "All right. I can understand that."

"Can we just forget about it right now?"

"I'm incapable of forgetting it, but I'll shut up. For now."

He climbed back into bed, snuggling up to her back. He kissed her neck. Something had changed within her now that he knew her origins. She didn't want him touching her, polluting himself with her disgusting flesh. She moved away from him.

"What's wrong?"

"I don't want to make love. I don't want you to touch me again until my slave mark is gone."

He wrapped his arms around her, turning her to face him and brought her on top of him. "I'll hold my lust in check, but you can't ask me not to touch you. I need to feel you next to me. Your skin, your pulse. We've been apart for far too long. Asking me to stop breathing would be a more reasonable request."

She laid her head on his chest, listening the steady rhythm of his heart. It was healthy and intact, while hers tore and crumbled around the edges.

Forest fell asleep on Syrus' chest. He lay awake, slashed by the heartache she transferred to him.

Chapter Thirteen

Sleep did not come easily to Syrus. When he finally did nod off, his dreams were filled with bloody images of killing Leith with his bare hands. He woke before the dawn, Forest still sprawled across his chest, a cute little wheezy snore coming from her nose when she exhaled. He shifted her to the side and got up. He wanted to go and talk to his father, but he didn't want Forest to wake up alone.

He dressed plainly for the day and ran his fingers through his cropped hair. It would take forever to grow back, he mused. He strapped on his belt with his flask that was running grievously low. He needed fresh human blood, but the portals were shut, and the ogres refused to open anything without Rahaxeris' say so. And it seemed that the elf had left the castle or was possibly ghosting around the place invisible.

Syrus was more uneasy about the High Priest being Forest's father than he cared to admit. What she'd told him about her origins bothered him even more. Not just because the news had sent her into a tailspin but how she didn't see it as others would. The balance of power had not shifted, it had broken. And Syrus could see how the *Rune-dy* would quickly be accepted as the authority of Regia. Forest was the daughter of the strongest being in their world. If and when it became public knowledge, she would be considered more royal than any other princess had ever been. They would see *him* as the grasping social climber trying to achieve her level rather than the other way around. He was a broken cripple from an overthrown monarchy, and she was engineered as a new and superior species.

Syrus shook his head in wonder and blew out a breath. My, my, how things were changing. Maybe Forest only needed time to adjust. Maybe…but so far she wasn't coping.

Syrus stood at the window, running his hands along the chiseled rocks of the frame. Strange. This was his home, but this wasn't the room of his childhood. The movements through the castle were foreign to him now. The sounds and people, different. Where did he fit? With Regia in transition, he could reinvent himself, if he wanted to. What did he want? He knew, deep down, but what about what others wanted from him: his father, the people, Redge…Forest?

The smell of the coming sunrise invigorated Syrus. He toyed with the flask for a moment, deliberating. He could use his incantation to restore his sight partially but he really hated doing that because it was so disorienting. Blurry and fragmented. Blood was required for clarity. Desperately wanting to see the sunrise and the beauty of the day's first light caressing Forest's skin, Syrus decided to drink the last of his human blood. The pain tore through him like a broken blade, twisting, stabbing, rending, and burning until it pushed through his eyes and his pupils stretched open.

He braced his hands on the window, panting and looked at the sunrise for one second before turning to gaze upon the only real sun in his world, Forest. He knelt next to the bed, much as he had the first time he'd looked at her. And just as it had the first time, again her beauty stole his breath. This pure, fierce, fragile beauty, her true face, his sole possession, that no one else could see.

Syrus gently smoothed a strand of hair from her face. "You don't know, do you?" he whispered, "Just how special you are. Or what I would do for you. How you torment me. Tempt me. Make me burn."

As he had done the first time, Syrus lifted a handful of her long curly hair and brought it to his lips. "I love you…with all that I am or ever hope to be." He couldn't wait any longer. His vision would fade all too quickly, and he had to look into her eyes. He hovered over her, his lips a breath from hers. "Forever," he breathed and pressed his lips against hers, waking her with a kiss.

The world of her eyes opened to him and shot through his core. Eye contact, so rare for the two of them, sent a jolt to both of their hearts. Nothing existed, just them. All worries forgotten as they sank into each other, the barriers were torn slowly, so slowly away.

****

Never had Forest experienced anything to rival the slow love they made that morning. Intensity without end and no inclination to hurry. Syrus said nothing to her with words, only his eyes. Her spirit rose through her skin as he worshiped her, yes worship was what it was. And after he took her there, to the edge of what was physically possible, he pushed her even higher and threw her into oblivion where she knew nothing but the depth of his love for her.

She rested her forehead against his, watching his eyes slowly begin to close. *No. Keep looking at me, Syrus.* The last moment sped by too quickly as his pupils dissolved into the pearl gray of his irises. And as his vision faded so did the warm wonderment of her afterglow.

Forest pulled away from him and into herself, feeling as through mud spread through her body just under her skin. She pulled the cover up over herself, not wanting to see her own flesh. "I told you I didn't want to make love until I was free of my slave mark."

Syrus chuckled, not taking her seriously. "Well, there's that saying about actions speaking louder than words..." he sobered. "I forgot. It seems you did too. I won't apologize, Forest, not for something so beautiful."

"Beautiful?" she spat getting out of bed and wrapping herself in a robe, only to sink onto the floor the next moment, weeping. "I ruin everything."

Syrus came to her and clasped her shoulders bracingly. "Stop it!" he ordered.

"I ruin everything," she repeated, "because I am ruin. Dross, worthless...I shouldn't even exist. I don't deserve your love."

Syrus lifted her chin, anger pulling through the muscles of his face. "I know I can't stop you from feeling something, but don't you ever say that to me again."

Forest jerked her face out of his grasp. "Don't touch me. I'm another man's slave."

Syrus grabbed her by the shoulders again. "Dammit, Forest!" he shouted. "Where the hell is this coming from? You're no man's slave, especially not that piece of shit's downstairs! That scar means nothing. It's just the illegitimate claim of a bastard, unworthy to kiss your feet."

She broke down crying.

"Let's get dressed and go take care of this once and for all."

"Huh?" she asked.

"Come on." He stood, offering her his hand. "Leith is waiting. We can do it together. Let's free you."

Forest didn't move to take his hand. "I want to kill him alone. I *need* to do it that way."

"Fine," he said testily, striding to the closet. "Do it by yourself. Just hurry up. I can't stand to be under the same roof as him much longer."

A sudden loud knock on the door jolted her to her feet. She wiped the tears from her cheeks and belted her robe. "Who is it?"

"Zeren," the king bellowed jovially.

"One moment." She looked at the closet door and Syrus came out fully clothed.

He strode to the door and opened it.

"Good morning!" Zeren exclaimed clapping Syrus on the shoulder. His happy expression faltered as his eyes fell on Forest. "Is everything all right? I could come back later."

"Everything's fine," Forest said quickly, forcing a smile.

"Good! Good." Zeren turned his attention solely to Syrus. "It's going to be a busy day. The officers are back, and there's going to be a war council in about an hour. I need you there, son. Much will be discussed. Important things. Visitors will be joining us, Fortress' high council, and the *Rune-dy*."

"But Father," Syrus protested. "I haven't even decided if I'm ready for the world to know I'm alive. I mean the high council knows but the officers don't."

Zeren waved away Syrus' concern loftily. "You have to come back to life some time. What better time than today?"

Syrus turned his face to Forest. "What do you think?"

"It's your choice," she said flippantly.

Syrus heard more than her words and almost smiled. Pissed off was way better than sad and crying. "Forest and I need to decide this together. Would you give us some privacy?"

"Of course." Zeren looked back at Forest. "Today will be busy for you too, my dear. We're going to have a state dinner tonight. All the highest-ranking vampires will be there. They're all anxious to meet my special guest." He winked at her conspiratorially. "Be sure to wear your best. They are unfortunately, a rather superficial bunch."

"But…" Forest panicked.

"Don't worry. If you need help getting ready, just send for a few handmaidens. Now that the queen is gone, they have nothing to do. I'm sure they'd be overjoyed to do your hair and make-up."

Forest's hands clenched into fists as Zeren left the room. Syrus laughed after he shut the door behind his father.

"What are you laughing at?" She demanded.

"I'm just picturing you being primped by a gaggle of my mother's old courtiers."

Forest gritted her teeth. "Hair and make-up, my ass."

Syrus pulled her into a tight hug. "Now you sound like the woman I fell in love with."

"Are you going to that meeting?"

"Do you think I should?"

"Well, one of us needs to know what is going on. But you don't have to go as yourself, you know?"

"You mean I should go in disguise?" he asked.

"Yeah. It might give you an edge, apart from holding off on letting the world know you're alive. Trust me. I know what it's like to glean information from people who don't know who they're talking to."

"You don't want people to know I'm alive?"

"I want it, if you want it. But once you let them know, you can't take it back."

Syrus looked thoughtful. "Hmm. True...I think I will wait a little longer."

"So you'll go to the meeting incognito?" she pushed.

"I guess so."

"Good. I really want to know what is going on."

"I'll tell you everything." He kissed her forehead. "I'm going to tell Redge the plan. I'll see you later."

"Okay," she said dejectedly to his retreating back. Then she was alone. The mock princess left waiting in her tower.

Chapter Fourteen

Forest paced down the center of the closet with a grimace on her face, the fabric of the hanging dresses brushing her shoulders. She didn't want to play dress up. She didn't want to play princess. She wanted to run away. Only her crushing resolve not to embarrass Syrus kept her from slashing the contents of the closet to ribbons. *Fine, fine, FINE!* If she had to dress up at least she'd force herself to find a dress she could stand to be seen in. She pushed down her ire and began really looking at her new clothes.

She designated a place on the rack to put dresses she knew she would *never* wear. Every article of clothing with any shade of pink went onto that rack, along with the overly sparkly, puffy sleeved, and anything with bows. Once she was done weeding, she found a few garments she could picture herself in, and three in particular she could almost get excited about: a liquid black dress that ran over her body like water, a green gown that matched her eyes and created the effect of a dragonfly, and lastly a red that blazed and danced like fire in the light. She decided to wear the red to the party and set her hair color to match. If she had to play the part, at least she could be intimidating in the role.

Forest stopped moving and stood stone still, an empty hanger clutched in her hands. *Role*, playing a *role*; that's what she'd been thinking. She clenched her teeth as her temper flashed. She was thinking about the whole thing all wrong, as if she was still a Fortress Operative and everything in front of her was simply an assignment to get through. She looked down at the hanger in her hands and snapped it. This was her life. If she chose wrong or if she failed, something far greater than a demotion was at stake. Her heart, soul, livelihood, reputation, and happiness shimmered in the distance. However, before she could grasp her desires, she must vault the hurdles at her feet.

She took a deep breath. Like it or not, this was her closet. These were her clothes. Well, acceptance didn't mean she couldn't change things to suit her better. She was a fighter, and she'd never stop fighting, but she could solider-on with more precision and less flailing.

Forest didn't hear the soft knock on the door, or the creak of the hinges when it was opened.

"Forest?"

She came out of the closet, still in her robe, and faced Rahaxeris. She hadn't expected to see him and took a second to school her expression and tone of voice. He held a large flat box in front of him.

"Ah, Daddy," she said in a sweet, mocking little girl way.

He smirked in response. "Here, put this on and be quick about it." He pushed the box into her arms.

"Now you're trying to dress me up, too? Is it something pretty to wear to the party?" Acid dripped through her tone.

Rahaxeris laughed, a frightening, terrible laugh. "Just open it."

Instead of a frilly dress, there was a plain black hooded robe inside, with long sleeves and a single *R* embroidered on the right breast in gold. "What is this for?"

"An important meeting is about to begin. This robe will mark you as my personal secretary so you may attend."

"The war council?"

"That's right."

"I don't think I was invited. I'm not supposed to…"

"Since when have you cared about following any rules? Smuggler." He smiled indulgently.

When she hesitated, he pushed. "Unless you'd rather get back to picking shoes to match your bag for this evening?"

Forest huffed. "Hell no. I'll be ready in a minute."

She quickly threw on the clothes she'd worn the day before and slid the robe on over the top. She regarded her appearance in the mirror for a second. She still had the same face she'd constructed for her first interview with her father.

"Should I change my face?" she asked as she came out of the bathroom.

"Well, that's up to you. I think you should consider picking a look you want the public to recognize. If you decide to accept the title of Hailemarris, or if you become queen, people will need some continuity from you."

Forest hesitated.

"I like this face. It seems…natural," Rahaxeris said.

"That's because it is very like my true face."

Rahaxeris smiled. "I'm sure Syrus must feel very lucky when he gets to look at you."

Forest could feel the pressure of oncoming tears, unsure why the pressure was there at all. Her father had paid her a compliment. He thought she was beautiful. Now more than ever, she was amazed that she could want his approval, but she did.

"How am I to behave in this meeting?"

"As my secretary, you'll not be expected to speak. Sit next to me on my left. Take notes."

"You want me to take notes?" Forest was incredulous.

"No, I don't care. Just look as though you're taking notes. I'll introduce you to the group."

Forest's eyes widened.

"Just as my secretary, not my daughter. Unless you've already decided to claim your birthright?"

"I haven't decided yet.'"

Rahaxeris shrugged but he didn't hide his disappointment. "Are you ready?"

****

Forest entered a large room that highly resembled a set for a movie about King Arthur. Tapestries lined the walls, depicting great Regian battles. The round table in the center of the room was massive, and its surface was painted with a map of the world. Security ogres stood at the only entrance, looking bored.

She stood close behind Rahaxeris, trying to look relaxed and right. The room was full of people, some she recognized, some she didn't. There were only two other women present, Gagnee and Zefyre from Fortress' high council. Forest spotted the other priests of the *Rune-dy,* murmuring to themselves in a corner, their golden robes providing the only color in the room as everyone else wore black. Her stomach gave a little jerk when she spotted Syrus, his face hidden in the shadow of a hood. His lips tightened as she looked at him. Of course he knew she was there, he could smell her. *Was he upset at her?* Zeren mingled around his glowering officers, who seemed resolved to snub the elves.

"This is quite a turn of events, isn't it?" a familiar voice said behind her.

Forest turned to see Kindel smiling at her. Never had she been so happy to see him and barely refrained from hugging him. "It's good to see you," she said emphatically.

"And you. Look at you! Back from banishment and on top of the world." He gestured to the gold R on her lapel. "Being declared princess isn't enough for you, eh? Got to stick your nose in politics, too."

Forest snorted. "Keep your voice down. I haven't been declared anything."

"Yet," Kindel added slyly.

Forest sighed. "Right."

"I've got to get back to my side of the table. Can we talk later?"

"Definitely."

A nervous quiet settled over the room as Rahaxeris was noticed. All eyes turned on him.

Zeren came forward. "Gentlemen, and ladies, we are all here now. Let us sit and discus the future of our great world."

Chairs scraped the floor. Forest sat on Rahaxeris' left as he had told her to. Zeren sat on the other side, directly across, with Syrus a few seats down from him looking withdrawn and unimportant. No one seemed to notice him. Forest tried not to stare.

"Not everyone is acquainted," Zeren announced. "Let us make introductions. First, I'm sure all of you who have regularly sat at this table with me have noticed the addition of our friends, the *Rune-dy*."

A murmur of assent went around the table.

"Let us all welcome them as brothers. Please stand and introduce yourselves."

As High Priest, Rahaxeris went first. He rose fluidly from his chair and gave a little bow to the room. "Thank you, Zeren. I am Rahaxeris, High Priest of the *Rune-dy*. We are honored to be among you today. I know that change can be uncomfortable for some and is often met with resistance and suspicion. The *Rune-dy* has largely worked to benefit the overall well-being of Regia for centuries, and we have done so predominantly in the shadows. But no more. The time has come for more direct, transparent involvement on our part in the machinery of this world."

Forest looked at the faces of Zeren's officers. She could tell they were listening attentively. Every face held some level of resentment and all had traces of fear behind their eyes. As her glance roved around the table, she caught the eye of a few people: Kindel, who winked and gave her a little side smile, Zefyre, who looked nervous and quickly looked away, and one of Zeren's battle worn generals, who surveyed her with interest and masculine appreciation. Forest's eyes settled again on Syrus. Rahaxeris continued to speak, but his words faded into a murmur in the background until he touched her shoulder.

"And when I am not present, my secretary, Forest, will stand in my stead."

Forest hesitated a split second, unsure if she should stand or not and decided to just nod her head once in acknowledgment and respect to the room. She expected half the room to jump to their feet and demand that the abomination be removed from the room. But no one said anything.

Rahaxeris sat back down. Forest flushed with pleasure. They had all looked at her and accepted her presence immediately. She looked back at Syrus, a small smile playing around his lips, he could feel her delight.

Everyone talked. Forest didn't just appear to take notes, she *did* take notes. Her wrist cramped long before the meeting was over. And once it was done, she realized that there really wasn't much that had been discussed. It was more of a meet and greet than anything. But she was a part of it. Accepted, however reluctantly for some, but accepted nonetheless as a member of the group.

Zeren let his men know change was coming so they could brace for it.

In the last few minutes, Forest looked again at Syrus and realized that no one in the room could know what was coming because they, she and Syrus, hadn't yet figured it out. Excitement mingled with a crushing fear deep in her stomach. Responsibility, obligation, power. What she chose to do now affected everyone.

The second chair legs scraped the floor, Forest bolted from the room. She wasn't ready to meet these strangers personally. She ran back to the room she shared with Syrus, feeling as though she was going to explode into a million pieces.

****

Syrus came in a few minutes later. "You gave me quite a surprise, showing up like that." His voice was light but she could hear the edge underneath.

"It wasn't planned. After you left, Rahaxeris showed up here and offered me the opportunity to go with him."

"There was more than a little buzz about you. I had to remind myself that I was in disguise to keep from choking General Wragg, who already fancies himself in love with you. Then there was Lieutenant Gerhard who wouldn't shut up about the *Rune-dy's* insane hiring practices, and how we can't trust them because they employ trash Halflings."

The part of Forest that had been elated vaporized. She crossed the room and laid a hand on Syrus' cheek. "I'm so sorry…I…"

"Sorry? What are you sorry about?"

"I embarrassed you."

Syrus made a small growling sound in his throat. "I'm an idiot who needs to learn when to shut his mouth. I shouldn't have told you what anyone said…You didn't embarrass me. I just reacted badly to the shock of you being there…I was really so proud of you." He leaned in and kissed her forehead. "Brave girl, you faced them all down. Not that I expected any different. I've been by your side when you faced down werewolves, guardians, Philippe, and worst of all, a bratty vampire prince who had the hots for you from the first."

Forest chuckled. "Yes, you were definitely the worst." She pulled his face down to hers and kissed him. "I love you, Syrus," she whispered. "I don't ever want to shame you."

"You couldn't. Stop saying it."

"A lot is riding on our choices. We need to figure it out."

"Yeah," Syrus nodded gravely. "My father really wants me to step up and take the crown. He's putting the pressure on…but I think it might be the perfect time to let the kingdom go. A republic would be better for the people…but maybe you becoming the queen would help things more."

"Me?" she scoffed then drew in a deep breath. "You told me once that you didn't want to be king. Has that changed?"

"No…and yes. Sparring last night reminded me how much I want to dedicate myself to the Kata. I wish we had more time to catch our breath." He drew his arms around her and pulled her close. "I just want to go away with you and not worry about anything for a while."

"That would be nice. I wonder if—"

The loud knock on the door had Syrus swearing. "Who is it?" he shouted.

"Zeren."

Syrus sighed, let go of her, and opened the door.

"Hey, son, we need to talk."

"Now?"

"Yeah, now. Come on, it's important."

"Fine." Syrus didn't hide his weariness.

"Oh, Forest." Zeren turned his full attention onto her. "I've gathered up every one of Christiana's handmaidens and told them they'll be serving you this evening. They should be up in about an hour."

Forest's forced smile felt as though it would break her face. "Thank you." *If you weren't Syrus' father, I'd shoot you in the knee.*

Syrus swept her up in a tight hug. "I'll see you later," he whispered in her ear, "as a free woman. Now would be a good time to take care of that."

She didn't reply. She stared at the closed door after Syrus and Zeren left, once again wishing she could run away. Her eyes slid out of focus as she ran her finger down the length of her scar. It felt strange, just a straight line now that the seven lovers marks were gone. What was wrong with her? Why did she hesitate on the threshold of freedom? Why did she feel unworthy of happiness?

Chapter Fifteen

Leith's eyes rolled, unfocused. Fragments of memories, not his own, flashed in his mind. He saw his own face over and over and heard Forest's cries of pain, felt them, uttered them. In his delirium, he tried to fend himself off. Various moments of brutality he'd subjected Forest to over the years melded together inside him. Sweat poured down his skin as he came back to himself, shaking back to his own thoughts. He felt no revelations or remorse, only hatred and confusion. The thorns moved slowly up, impeding the blood flow in his arms. He thought of Forest, felt her draw near.

****

Forest's left hand rested on the hilt of her sword while the right clenched around the key to Leith's cell. She felt numb. Not at all like the last time she'd had him pinned. Nothing could save him now, he couldn't escape.

The magic responded to the key as she slid it into the lock.

Leith sat on the floor in the far corner of the empty room. His head, resting against the stone wall, lifted and slowly turned toward her. His eyes were bloodshot and his skin looked waxy. The flesh on his forearms held the appearance of necrosis spreading up from his wrists.

"Forest? Is it you, Forest?"

"Yes." Her voice was flat. "What happened to you?"

He heaved a great sigh, as though he was too weak to answer. "Some elf put me here, and he gave me these." Leith lifted his arms, giving her a better view of his wounds.

Forest didn't move any closer to inspect him. "What is that doing to you?"

He shrugged. "Punishment. And now here you are, ready to kick me when I'm down." His watery eyes drifted over the hand that gripped her sword. "Or have you come to rescue me?"

When she made no reply or move, he looked away from her and leaned his head back against the wall. "You can't help yourself. I made sure of that all those years ago. Like it or not, you love me."

Forest took one step toward him then crouched down to his level.

"What are you doing?" he asked when she pulled a small knife out of her boot.

"I want you to see something."

She took the blade and slit open the shoulder and arm of her sleeve. He blinked a few times looking where the lovers marks used to mar her skin, abruptly he closed his eyes, tears running down his cheeks.

"Who is he?" Leith hissed.

"What does it matter?"

Leith sat up a little, a small surge of energy animating him. "I'd kill him…if I could. For taking what's mine." He slumped back breathing heavily. "You are still mine. Your slave mark is still there."

"For the moment."

"Come closer," he ordered.

Forest wasn't prepared to fight off commands and obeyed before she could stop herself. He reached up and pulled her into a crouch beside him. Quicker than she gauged he was able; his hand shot out and thrust roughly between her legs. Forest surged backward, light flashing off the small blade as it slashed diagonally across Leith's pretty face, splashing a line of blood on her chest. Leith covered his face with his hands, screaming.

She stood up, wiping the blade on her jeans.

Forest sneered and spat on him. "I was going to kill you," she said loudly over his cries. "But *I'm* using *you* now. So for the time being, I'll delight in the extra pain I've given you, while you buy me some more time."

"FOREST!"

His screaming vibrated through the door as she closed and locked it, the magic pulling back together over the wood. The protection muffled the sound, but it could still be heard. Forest hung the key back around her neck and stalked down the hall. The warm blood on her clothes caused the fabric to cling to her skin. She smiled at the sensation and quickly headed back to change, unaware that anyone had seen her.

****

"You've got to be kidding."

A mob of eager handmaidens crowded at the door. Their puffy sleeves and skirts packed around them as they pushed together to get a good look at their new mistress. They looked like a set of china dolls in a packing crate to Forest. She bit down on her tongue and took a deep breath, looking at their powdered expectant faces. They curtsied in perfect formation.

"All right, who of you has the..." Forest strained to think of the right words. "...The highest rank?"

"I do, mistress."

Forest scowled at the face right in front of her. "Would you please point out whom here has the lowest rank?"

"Of course, mistress." The painted doll turned around and pointed a finger at a bowed head in the back. "Her. Ena."

The ocean of crinoline and silk parted to give Forest a clear view of Ena. Her light brown hair was braided simply, and her grey dress was plainer than the others around her. Ena curtsied, keeping her eyes on the floor, her cheeks flushed with pink. Forest looked back to the painted doll. "Why does she have the lowest rank?"

The doll lifted her pointed chin arrogantly. "Weak bloodlines, and she's trouble. It's probably her lack of breeding that makes her so stupid."

All the other dolls giggled. Forest looked back at Ena. Rage clearly boiled under her flushed skin but she remained silent.

"Ena, please come inside." Forest stepped aside in the doorway so Ena could enter the room. "The rest of you are fired."

"But mistress!" The highest ranking came forward. "I served Christiana for years. She always said I was her favorite."

"Really?" Forest sneered. "Maybe firing you isn't enough. Perhaps I shall have the ogres put you under arrest."

All the dolls gasped.

"Now scram before I take my sword to your skirts."

"Just who do you think you are?" screamed the doll. "I can trace my lineage back six centuries."

"That's nice," Forest said sharply. "I'm the bastard child of two races. And I have a party to get ready for. So get out of my sight and stay out." Forest gave them all a broad grin. "Welcome to the new world order."

She slammed the door in their shocked faces. Forest turned to the young woman behind her. Ena held her hand over her mouth, making a small noise that sounded like a gasp and a giggle mixed. Her bronze eyes grew wide, and she curtsied again as Forest took a step toward her.

"Milady," Ena said quietly.

"So, Ena, with the lowest rank." Forest smirked. "Now, with the highest. I'll let you know now that I don't desire servants. I've been grooming myself my whole life, and I certainly don't need some sniveling china doll helping me put my butt into my skivvies."

Ena snorted, flushed, and curtsied again. "Yes, Milady."

Forest softened her tone. "How long did you serve Christiana?"

"Three years, Milady."

"Where were you before that?"

"At home with my family. I was sent to the castle when I came of age," Ena said dispassionately.

"Are you happy here?"

Ena's eyes grew fearful.

"You can tell me the truth. I don't care if you hate it here."

"I *do* hate it, Milady... This is not what I had envisioned for my life. I want to travel. I want to start a family of my own, with a man I choose, not one from the right bloodlines. I want…I'm sorry. I've spoken too much."

Forest regarded the young woman.

"I'm very happy to serve you, Milady. You have already made my life so much better."

Forest smiled. "Don't get ahead of yourself. Those spiteful peacocks still live in the castle. I'd watch my back for reprisals, if I were you."

"But I'm with you. And you're with that *Rune-dy,* aren't you? They're too scared of him to do anything."

Forest hoped for her sake, Ena was right.

Ena abruptly got down on both knees and grabbed Forest's hand. "I pledge to you my undying loyalty, Milady."

"Uhh…thanks. Get up, we're running out of time. Can you do my hair the way a queen would wear it?"

"Oh, yes! Hair is what I do best." Ena walked around Forest, her bottom lip caught between her sharp teeth. "Pity yours isn't six inches longer, I could do the most intricate design. No matter, there's enough for…"

"Six more inches?" Forest asked, forcing her hair to lengthen. "Or would eight be better?"

"Ooooh!" Ena exclaimed bouncing on the balls of her feet. "Wow. Just you wait till I'm finished!" She began running her fingers through Forest's hair, separating it into sections. "Wait, does your dress go over your head?"

"Um. Not sure."

Forest showed Ena her dress selections. Ena agreed fervently that she must wear the red, but it didn't have to go over her head, so it could wait till her hair was finished.

Forest didn't enjoy the styling as Ena pulled and threaded, braided and curled, but she suffered in silence, allowing the young woman to enjoy herself. And she couldn't deny the end result was "queenly."

This is stupid. Why are you doing this? Forest asked herself. *Syrus. You're doing it for Syrus.*

Forest gritted her teeth as she slipped her arms through the sleeves of the fire dress. Despite her big talk about not needing help getting dressed, she did have Ena lace up the back.

"You look amazing, Milady! More beautiful than Christiana ever did."

Forest took a deep breath. "Thank you, Ena. I appreciate it. It's important that I don't look out of place tonight."

"Oh, you won't! Not at all. You shall set a new standard."

"Great," Forest grumbled. "Just what I was going for."

****

Syrus rolled his neck and stood up. "I'm sorry. Maybe if everyone would leave us alone longer than three minutes, Forest and I could have a real discussion about it. At this moment, I can't say one way or the other, Father."

Zeren knew he was pushing too hard, but he couldn't seem to stop himself. It wasn't that he didn't see the possible benefit of Regia becoming a republic. He just wanted to see his son on the throne. He had wanted it ever since Syrus had been born. Zeren knew it was in Syrus to be a much better king than he had been.

"All right," Zeren said. "I'll not ask you again. I'll just wait for your answer."

"Thanks. I really appreciate what you're planning to do for Forest tonight, and as much as I'd love to be there, I think it best if I don't show up."

"Why?"

"Stop playing stupid, Father. I can see your plan. I'm not ready to come back from the dead. I don't want all those people to see me."

"You could go in disguise again," Zeren suggested. "It will be a shame if you miss it."

"It is a shame, but our connection is too new. If Forest is in the same room, I cannot help but be next to her. I can't stop from touching her. And all eyes will be on her tonight."

"How do you think she will take it?" Zeren asked.

"No idea. But she's tough. She can handle anything."

Zeren stood up and placed a hand on Syrus' shoulder. "I'm glad you have her. Don't ever let anything separate you. Losing your mate is a pain no heart should have to bear."

"Father?"

"My obligation as king is what killed my mate."

"What?" Syrus knew there was no way Zeren was speaking of Christiana.

Zeren took a deep breath. "I've never told you about Phippa, but I think it's time…I sealed my bond with Christiana one year after taking the throne because I caved to pressure. She was of the right bloodline, and she manipulated me completely. At first, I thought she loved me. But she loved nothing but power. She was pregnant with you when I met Phippa….

"Phippa had been employed in the kitchens; she was serving that night…Our eyes met. She dropped the tray she was carrying. No one in the room noticed what had really happened. I couldn't make her the queen. Removing Christiana was impossible since she was pregnant. And as soon as Christiana learned of it…well, you know your mother…I wasn't strong enough…I didn't do all I could. Phippa waited for me, but when I was called away Christiana forced her out of the castle and…" Zeren turned away from Syrus, wrapping his arms around his torso. "I'm sorry…I've never spoken of it."

It was Syrus' turn to put his hand on his father's shoulder. "It's all right. If it's too painful."

"Oh, it is son," Zeren's voice broke. "The pain never stops. My heart never stops beating, but it's just a lump of dead tissue. If it weren't for you, I'd have died right along with her."

"If it weren't for me?"

"Of course. You'll understand when you have a child. I couldn't leave you. You were, *are* my reason for living. But you must do everything you can to keep Forest with you. I can't stand the idea of you suffering the same loss that I have."

At his father's words, Syrus felt a great weight settle into his heart. Forest would never want a child, he was sure of it. She wouldn't be able to stand the idea of mixing even more bloodlines. And maybe she was right. A child of three races was, as far as he knew, an unprecedented entity.

Wanting to shrug off the solemnness of their conversation, Syrus abruptly cleared his throat. "I think it's about time for the party to start. You should go down."

"Yes, you're right. The time draws near."

Chapter Sixteen

Forest waited, not moving much, as she feared she would come apart, ruin her hair, or tear her dress. She thought Syrus would be back before the party.

"Is there anything else I can do for you, Milady?" Ena asked.

"No. Thank you. You can go now."

Ena curtsied and headed for the door.

"Ena, wait."

"Yes, Milady?"

"You said you wanted to travel."

Ena's brows came together. "Yes, Milady. I do."

"Why don't you?"

Ena hesitated a moment. "Well, I can't. My life is in service."

Forest crossed her arms. "Are you telling me you're a slave?"

"Uh, well. I don't think about it in those terms. I find the word 'slave' offensive."

Forest smiled a little. "So do I."

Ena shifted a little, looking uncomfortable.

"Thank you for being candid, Ena. You may go."

Ena curtsied again and left.

Forest sighed and rubbed her temple, a headache pinching just beneath the surface. She looked out the window at the sunset spreading over the land. She could see so much: The sprawling vampire city of Halussis, the edge of Paradigm, and the Fortress castle, the mountains and forests, and her heart ached to go home.

She turned from the window and looked in the mirror. She might not look out of place, but her heart was shouting that she didn't and would never belong here. Her skin began to itch under the fabric of the dress, and her fingers curled into claws about to tear it all away. A sharp knock on the door stopped her.

She didn't get the chance to ask who it was.

"Forest, it's Zeren. I'm here to escort you to the party. May I come in?"

Forest relaxed her fingers. "Yes. Come in."

Zeren opened the door. Forest smiled unwittingly. Syrus looked so much like his father. Zeren wore a simple bronze crown that matched his breastplate, and a black cape fell around his shoulders.

He returned her smile and gave her a small bow. "You look beautiful, my dear. I wish Syrus could see you now."

"So do I," she said sadly.

"Come." He offered his arm.

She took it, feeling better as they walked down the halls, as though his arm gave her shelter. He smiled down at her again and squeezed the hand she rested on his arm with his other hand. The emotions filling her were warm and unfamiliar. He offered her support, protection, and approval.

They crossed under an archway into the party. The opulence gave Forest whiplash. She clenched her teeth together so her mouth wouldn't hang open in amazement. Everything was so bright and sparkly, her vision blurred, pockmarked, where the light had burned her retina. She stared at the chandelier, unconscious irritation rising up her throat. She knew enough of Christiana to know that every gem and bauble that caught the light was real. Forest wanted to tear the thing from the ceiling, sell it off piece-by-piece, and give the money to the poor and hungry.

Zeren led her to the head of a massive table. All faces turned to her with interest. Zeren pulled out her chair and everyone rose to his or her feet, waiting for her to be seated. She expected them to sit again after she had, but they remained standing.

"My lords and ladies," Zeren greeted everyone in a bellowing voice. "I am honored for you all to meet The Lady Forest, my adopted daughter, and heir."

Every face mirrored her own with wide-eyed shock.

"Let us all lift a glass to The Lady Forest," Zeren commanded, picking up a goblet.

Everyone copied his action, their shock sliding back into smiles. As soon as Zeren drank, everyone else did too. The men pounded on the table in approval after the toast. Forest lifted her own glass in a toast to everyone in the room and took a deep gulp, hoping desperately whatever was inside was strong enough to make her drunk.

Zeren clapped his hands loudly, bringing in an army of servants with dinner trays. Forest focused all of her mind on the herculean task of getting through dinner without making a fool of herself. *It's just a job. The spy gig Fortress never gave you.*

With that thought lodged firmly in her mind, she smiled regally at everyone and took another drink. The wizened duke next to her leaned in, kissed her hand, and introduced himself. She heard everything and nothing at the same time. She flirted, teased, and insulted everyone as only aristocracy can. Dinner was the best Regian food she had ever tasted, but she acted as though it was hardly worth consuming. The more superior she behaved, the more Zeren beamed at her across the table.

When dinner was finished and dessert was brought in, Forest was beginning to enjoy herself. The vampires now filled their glasses with blood and just to mess with them, she asked for blood as well.

"But you're not a vampire, Milady," the Duke protested, aghast.

Forest took a small sip and smiled teasingly at him, her teeth crimson. "Do you really know *what* I am?"

He blinked a few times and turned his face back to his plate, obviously offended and embarrassed.

Talk around the table turned political. Zeren caught Forest's eyes and shook his head slightly. The next second he stood up dramatically, walked to Forest's chair, and lifted her hand. "Friends, tonight is not for talk of worries and wars. Tonight we celebrate." He gave them all a wicked smile. "Tonight, we dance."

Applause erupted around the room as a troupe of musicians filed in. Zeren led her to the dance floor as the musicians began playing an ancient formal song. Forest didn't have to worry about the steps, all she had to do was hang on as Zeren waltzed her around. When the song changed, she found herself passed off to another partner, and then another. Their faces hazed together until they all melded into one gross blob. She had looked at too many faces that night, and she hated them all because none of them was Syrus.

The whole charade blurred like an odd dream that could turn into a nightmare at any second.

****

Confusion turned into sorrow. Sorrow gave birth to pain. Pain painted long gashes through Syrus' inner darkness. *Why? Why was Leith still alive?*

Syrus' hands braced on the magic that barred him from Leith. He could feel the blackguard's life force behind the door. Still alive. Breathing. And keeping Forest from fully being his. Why hadn't she finished him? The gashes of pain began to crackle red with the rage Syrus desperately fought to hold back. His mind had to be clear. He must grab a hold of the understanding that danced just beyond his reach.

"Syrus?" Redge came up behind him.

Syrus took a deep breath. "Leith is still alive. I can feel him. I don't know why Forest hasn't come here and..."

"She has."

Syrus turned on Redge. "What?"

"She came to see him a few hours ago. I wasn't following her, Syrus. It was just coincidence. But she left the door open and I heard. I'm sorry."

Syrus waved Redge's apology away. "What did you hear?"

Something inside Redge clinched, and he desperately wished he wasn't compelled to tell Syrus.

"Well, they talked, nothing much. His was just postulating. He wanted to know who her new lover was. She didn't tell him. There was some scuffling, and then she injured him in some way because he started screaming. Then she told him she would use him to buy some time. Then she left, blood all over her clothes."

Syrus gave Redge a brotherly pat on the arm. "Thanks." There seemed to be no life in his voice. "I need to be alone for a while."

Redge watched sadly as Syrus walked away, down the dark hall.

****

Forest hadn't turned in so many consecutive circles since she'd been a child. Amazingly, she managed not to get sick to her stomach. The waltz ended, and her partner released her and kissed her hand before walking away. She took a deep breath as her equilibrium tried to right itself. The musicians began playing again, making Forest curse in her head. She wanted to be done with the party.

Her next partner swaggered toward her, causing her brain to trip. Before she could gasp, Leith caught her in a harsh grasp and began spinning her around the floor.

No. Not Leith, his twin, Lorcan. She struggled against him as he crushed her against his chest.

"Well, well, well. If it isn't my brother's whore," he whispered in her ear, lewdly licking her lobe. "Seduced the king with those sorceress eyes, have you? I'm impressed."

Forest clenched her teeth, unsure what to do. She could beat the hell out of him, but everyone would see. Maybe she could just act the girl and scream. "What do you want, Lorcan?" she hissed.

"I want my brother. I know you've done something with him."

"I *have* done something with him. I killed him."

Lorcan flinched before schooling his face into a sneer. He squeezed her tighter, making it hard to breathe.

"Think, Lorcan. I'm now Zeren's daughter. I'll have your head for this."

"Zeren has lost his mind, all the nobility think so. None of us will bow to a disgusting abomination like you. In fact, once we lock Zeren up and throw away the key, I'm going to claim you as my own, and the time you spent with Leith will seem like heaven compared to the hell I'll put you through."

"Get your filthy hands off me!" Forest shrieked.

"Is there a problem here?" Zeren asked, placing a firm hand on Lorcan's shoulder.

Lorcan let go of Forest and took a step back, a nasty smile curling his lips. The people around them stopped dancing and were watching them.

"Shall I tell him about you, Forest? Or would you like to do the honors?"

A shot of ice went straight to Forest's stomach. She didn't want Lorcan telling Zeren or anyone else in the room, anything about her past. She shot a panicked glance at Zeren.

"You can leave now, Lorcan. Or, I'll have you escorted out." Zeren waved his hand, and an ogre was instantly at his side.

Lorcan continued to smile, but he backed away. "Just wait," he said to the room in general. "Wait till you learn the truth about *the Lady Forest*." He turned and quit the room.

Every eye was stuck on Zeren and Forest and she desperately wished the music was still playing, but even the musicians were looking intently at her.

"I...I'm sorry," she stammered. "I've known Lorcan many years." She tried to smile, thinking quick. "I broke his heart as a boy, at academy. He's never forgiven me."

Many faces smiled and winked. Some chuckled and looked back to their dance partners. Forest looked pleadingly at Zeren again. He nodded and gestured for the music to resume.

Forest looked toward the doorway where Lorcan had just left. "I have some business to attend to, Zeren. I need a sword."

Zeren swept her up into a dance again. "No, Forest. You are to be the queen. Queen's don't take up swords and chase down their enemies to kill them in the streets."

"But..."

"No," Zeren said firmly. "Hard as it may be, you must be still and wait. Leave it to other's to handle."

"Fine," she snapped. "Let me go tell some others so they can take care of it. If he isn't silenced quickly, he will do irreparable damage to me. Please."

"Calm down. I'll have him brought in for questioning first thing in the morning."

"That's not good enough!"

Zeren looked exasperatedly down at her. "I'll end the party, and we can talk about this some more."

He danced her around the floor for the rest of the song. *What kind of nonsense is this?* She wondered. Dancing as though nothing was wrong. Smile, chat, and be charming when she should have been standing over Lorcan's corpse. Let someone else handle it—to hell with that. Killing vampire scum was what she did best. She still held the traffic controller kill record in Fortress and would for some time to come. But she held still and did as Zeren told her, while bloodlust coated her mouth.

****

Syrus stopped dead in his tracks, feeling the murder Forest was longing for, transfer into him. He'd paced the perimeter of the courtyard nearly fifty times, letting the night air soothe him. But now he stood stone still, trying to dissect the emotion he picked up from her.

He shadowed himself as someone else walked into the courtyard, muttering under their breath.

"*Halfling.* I know Leith is here. I'm his twin after all. I can feel it…just wait…oh, I'll make her pay…everyone will know she's a slave whore…everyone…"

Syrus now felt his own desire for blood. He cleared his throat loudly and shuffled his feet. Lorcan whirled around. "Hello?"

"Good evening," Syrus said silkily.

Lorcan's eyes darted around. "Uh. I can't see you."

"I know. I'm not really alive."

Lorcan arched a brow. "A ghost?"

Syrus plowed his fist into Lorcan's gut, doubling him over. "No. Not a ghost."

Lorcan sucked the air in, sharply straightening back up. "What are you then?" he demanded in a wheeze.

Syrus stepped right in front of Lorcan and un-shadowed. "I'm your death."

Lorcan stumbled back in surprise, blinking a few times. "It can't be…" he said, looking intently. "Syrus? It can't be you. You're dead."

Syrus smiled. "No, *you're* dead." He stepped forward.

"Wait! What did I ever do to you? We're kin."

"Gah, don't remind me. As to what you've done. You've done plenty, and more than enough to my mate, Forest."

Lorcan watched in horror as Syrus' rage rose through his skin. Red lightening dazzled his eyes a second before the pain slid under his skin. Syrus left Lorcan's body where it fell on the ground and went back into the castle.

Chapter Seventeen

Ending the party was a bigger fiasco than the dinner and dancing put together. No one seemed willing to leave, even when Zeren was being more than a little obvious that it was time for them to go. Forest waited to talk to him as he had instructed, but as the last few stragglers filed out, an overdressed peacock grabbed him by the arm and vociferously demanded to speak with him in private.

"I can't now, Dracula. We can talk tomorrow," Zeren said.

Dracula puffed his chest up. "With all due respect, Your Highness. What I have to say will not keep."

Zeren sagged and gave Forest an apologetic look. "I'll be back in a minute."

As soon as they were out of sight, Forest took off through a side door, hoping she could find someone with a sword and take off after Lorcan. She turned a corner and skidded to a halt. Syrus was at the other end of the hallway, coming toward her. Satisfaction radiated from him and slid into her, easing her desire to kill.

His expression changed from jubilation to pain as he caught her scent. He said nothing, but took her hand as he walked past and pulled her along after him.

His pain hurt her. *Why did he feel like this?* She wondered.

They walked in silence, winding their way through the castle back to their room. Everything felt broken. The party had been exhausting and frighteningly eye-opening. Lorcan was loose, wielding her past as a weapon against her. A throne loomed before her, hands pushing her toward it. Rahaxeris offered her a title. An unhappy servant had styled her hair. Leith waited in his cell below. And Syrus... Syrus deserved better.

It was too damn much. Forest was screaming inside.

Syrus closed their door and bolted it. The silence hung between them, heavy and thick. The hurt pulsing through him, sliding into her, made her nauseated.

"I just killed Lorcan," Syrus said abruptly. "In the courtyard. Someone will have stumbled across his body by now, I expect."

Forest's breath came out in whoosh. "Oh, well. Thanks. That's great." A momentary relief filled her.

His lips pulled back into a smile that was nothing short of scary. "It was a pleasure. It's really too bad Leith's body can't be thrown on the garbage pile along with him."

"Oh...I didn't have the time, with the party prep-"

"Don't," Syrus cut her off sharply. "Don't lie to me. I can't even fathom why you feel you need to."

"How do you know I was lying?"

"You were overheard."

Forest's throat clenched.

Syrus shook his head. "Please explain this to me, Forest. I don't understand..." He rubbed the heel of his hand over his heart. "...I cannot comprehend these feelings coming from you."

"I just..." Words failed her. She closed her mouth, unable to form coherent sentences. Her heart pounded violently under her ribs.

"You don't want to be the queen."

"No, I don't," she said quietly. "I'm sorry."

"What, you think that's a big surprise to me?" He shot back acidly.

"I thought maybe you wanted it. I wanted to try for you."

His face softened. "Oh, baby..." He reached for her, but she backed away. "Back to this again are we, Forest? You don't want me to touch you until your mark is gone, but you won't do what needs to be done to remove it. You know what that tells me?"

Syrus gasped loudly in pain and clutched at his chest. "My heart reads yours clearly. It doesn't matter what you say, your heart tells mine the truth…You don't want to be my mate."

Forest had no words. Her tears fell silently. What he said was both true and untrue, but she couldn't contradict him.

"This can't be broken, Forest!" He pointed to her and back at himself. "Except by death. Is that what you want? You want me dead?"

"NO!" Forest's voice came back sharply. "Never."

"But you choose pain over joy."

"I guess I do," she whispered.

He lifted his chin and pulled his shoulders back. "Tell me the truth. What do you want?"

"I need some time…to figure everything out."

"And you want space from me?"

Forest wiped at her tears. "Yes." She could barely hear her own voice.

"Fine," he snapped. "You'll have both time and space. I'm leaving."

"Where?"

"I'm going to the Obsidian Mountain where the masters of the Blood Kata go to train. At least I'll be *useful* there."

A small snapping pain flicked around the edges of Forest's heart. *No, Syrus. Please don't leave me! I'm sorry. We'll figure this out, together. I love you…I love you.*

The words never made it past her lips.

He turned his back and opened the door. His whole torso crumpled the next second, and he turned back to her, once again clutching his chest. A single tear ran down his cheek. "Is this my heart breaking, or yours?" he gasped.

Both.

Syrus inhaled sharply and straightened. "Just mine then... Farewell, Forest. My love, the murderer of my soul."

The door shut behind him.

Nothing and everything. That's what she felt—nothing and everything. How could she have ever thought she wanted to let him go? Yet she had.

A small voice began to panic in her head. *No! What are you doing? Don't just stand there! Run! Catch him. Stop him. Don't let him go!*

"Syrus, wait!" Forest bolted out of the room and into the hall. It was empty and silent. She looked one way and the other, but he was gone.

"Syrus," she cried. Her voice echoed through the vacant halls as she sank to the floor, cursing herself, her heart pulling taut, rending jaggedly down the center. Her mind went blank as her forehead pressed against the stone floor. Her eyes blurred out of focus.

She may have stared at the floor minutes or days, she didn't know. But the world around her came back as someone grasped her shoulders and forced her to sit up. Forest blinked a few times, looking into the concerned face of Zeren. He looked so much like Syrus; she reached out and wrapped her arms around his neck. He patted her back, as a father would comfort his little girl.

"Forgive me, Forest," Zeren said quietly. "I don't know you at all. I should have taken the time to fix that."

"It's just too much," she sobbed. "I can't think, and now Syrus is gone. I broke his heart and my own in the process, and now I am truly alone."

"No, no, no. It will be all right," he said bracingly. "Broken hearts are like wax, they fuse back together. All couples have trouble."

She could tell Zeren meant what he said, but his words seemed hollow. She pulled away from him and pushed her hair away from her face. "I can't stay here. I want to go home."

Zeren nodded gravely. "Okay. Just remember, this is your home now, too. And you have family here."

Forest looked at him confusedly for a moment before she realized the family he spoke of was himself. She managed a small smile. "Thank you. If Syrus comes back, please tell him I went home to my cottage."

"I will."

Forest took her sword and traveling cloak and nothing else from the Onyx Castle. She thought about looking in on Leith before she left, but decided she couldn't handle it. The key around her neck felt heavier than ever.

Hoping a good walk would help clarify her thinking, Forest asked Merhl to open a portal a few miles outside of Anue, the town closest to her property. As she stepped into the portal, the cries of her heart ground to a dull moan, the steady pain preventing any thought or circumstance to bring solace to her wound.

I've lost everything.

No, I threw it away.

Chapter Eighteen

Netriet looked in at the fair from under the cover of trees. Raindrops slid down her face. Her gaze darted around suspiciously, as her mind grew more and more feral. She stayed away from people and civilization as a rule, but this place had drawn her. She'd watched the activity and the different kinds of people at the fair for two days without venturing any closer than she was right now. A small seed of hope had begun to open within her as she observed that possibly she had found a place she might be accepted. The people who lived in the brightly colored tents had formed their own society, despite that they all came from different racial backgrounds, misfits and dregs, creating happiness and peace out of sheer determination.

She listened to the talk. The world was in chaos. She'd walked right through it or around it. She'd stepped over bodies of those fallen in battle, left to rot in the open. The dead didn't bother her, the living, however repelled and caused her great disquiet. She couldn't trust her responses. She had no control over her emotions. Netriet knew that she was mentally unfit to be around people, but despite the fear they caused, she was lonely.

How long would she watch and wait? Would she ever make contact? Living a solitary life only made sense to her if she was doing good of some sort. Netriet doubted there was any good inside her at all. The darkness moved beneath her skin. The desire for goodness from other people writhed within her like a hunger. She must find a balance or else the darkness would consume her completely. She didn't want the sweet whisperings of hate, the caressing hands of jealousy, or the succulent lips of murder. The shadow inside begged to be her lover. She must not become the thing it promised to make her.

The rain turned to a bone-chilling fog as the evening descended. She decided to create a small camp for herself at the base of a large tree. Its branches touched the ground, creating a patchy umbrella over her. Her shelter provided privacy but little to no warmth. The change of clothes she carried in her pack was as dirty and wet as the ones she wore. She wished for a blanket or a cloak. Huddled against the tree trunk, her arm wrapped around her knees, she began to shiver, and for the first time in three days, she dozed off to sleep.

The sound of voices roused her. She listened to the tones, unable to hear the words. Tears blurred her eyes. The nuance of the conversation was friendly and joyful. Netriet unfolded herself and stood up, hunching under the boughs. Her whole body ached with the cold and from sleeping on the ground. She emerged from her cover, the smell of smoke drifting through the trees. There must be a fire with people standing around it, talking. The mental image seduced her completely, and she walked toward the sound of conversation without thinking.

Three people huddled around the fire. She observed them for a few minutes from the shadows. The woman's size made it obvious she was an ogre. A patched, brightly colored shawl hung on her broad shoulders. Her face seemed plain until she smiled. And when she laughed, Netriet was sure she'd never seen anyone so lovely. The ogre woman leaned over and planted a kiss on the gruff, cranky looking werewolf standing next to her. He muttered at her as though he didn't like it, causing her to laugh again, before he reached for her and kissed her back in a way that was unmistakably loving.

The other individual next to the fire was a thin vampire, absentmindedly juggling wooden balls, as if he was doing nothing more than twiddling his thumbs. The balls constantly rising and falling, passing through his hands, mesmerized Netriet. Each was inlaid with some kind of metal and the firelight glinted off them. She watched the juggler closely. He looked frail, which contrasted with his easy agility. He shared in the conversation infrequently. His eyes, trained on the fire, looked hollow. She saw him smile once, the wrinkles around his eyes denoting that he was approaching middle age.

She considered retreating to her tree just as the juggler's eyes snapped right onto hers. She gasped and took a step back. Should she run? All three of them were looking at her now.

"Hello there," the ogre lady said. "It's a cold night. Would you like to come closer to the fire? We won't harm you as long as you don't harm us."

She thought another second about running before taking a few steps out of the shadows, the warmth pulling her closer. They moved aside, giving her space to approach.

"Who are you?" the juggler asked firmly.

"Who are *you*?" Netriet shot back aggressively.

The werewolf threw his head back and laughed.

The juggler scowled. "*I* am a part of this community, and you are not. Declare yourself and state your business."

Netriet looked around anxiously, sensing she'd made a mistake that she might be welcomed here.

"Calm down," the ogre lady said. She gave Netriet a warm smile. "My name is Martia, and this is my mate, Tek. And cranky butt there is Merick."

"My name is…" She'd forgotten to decide on a new one yet. "Nettie," she said, using the nickname Philippe had given her.

"There's no heat on your tail is there?" Tek demanded.

Netriet didn't understand.

"You're not on the run? Being pursued?" he pushed.

She shook her head.

Martia snorted. "Ah, my love, you're such a hypocrite."

"What?" Tek said innocently.

"How many outstanding warrants are on your head?" she teased.

"That's different. No one cares about me. I just want to make sure she doesn't have a posse behind her."

"No one is following me. Everyone who used to know me thinks I'm dead." Netriet's voice sounded strange to her, not having used it in so long.

"What happened to your eye?" Merick asked.

Netriet had expected questions on how she lost her arm. Merick's question threw her. "My eye? Nothing happened to my eye." But she rubbed her fingers on her eyelids, checking. Everything felt fine. She looked questioningly at Martia.

The woman smiled sympathetically. "It's unique," she said kindly.

Netriet racked her brain. What was wrong with her eye? She needed a mirror. She thought she had seen every new deformity to her body, but apparently, she was wrong. She looked around at her companions, their gazes probing and curious. Abruptly Netriet turned on her heal and began to sprint away.

"Wait!" Martia called.

Netriet looked back, continuing to move away.

"Here. Take this to keep you warm." Martia held out her brightly colored shawl.

Netriet stopped, the patched fabric calling her back. Martia met her half way and tucked it snuggly around Netriet's shoulders. Tears pooled in her eyes as she realized she must reject the gift. "I'm sorry. I have nothing to pay you for it."

Martia shook her head and stopped Netriet's hand as she tried to pull the shawl from her shoulders. "All I ask as payment is that you come back and talk to me a little. I could use some female companionship."

"I'm afraid," Netriet confessed, her eyes darting back to the two men next to the fire.

"I understand. When you come back, if anyone stops or questions you, just say you are Martia's guest. You can always find me around the Human Relics tent. Promise you'll come back?"

Netriet nodded and backed away. Martia gave her a smile as warm as the fire and went back to stand beside her mate.

The night felt darker and colder as Netriet retreated into solitude. Martia's shawl warmed her, and she brushed her cheek against the fabric, taking comfort from it. It smelled like wood smoke and spices, and she sank into it as a child does a mother's embrace. She thought back to her life before she had been arrested and sent to Philippe. It was like watching someone else's dream, and she let it slip away, deciding she would never again try to recall any of it.

Her head pillowed on her pack, cocooned under her tree and wrapped in Martia's shawl, Netriet fell asleep wondering what her eyes looked like now.

The sounds of muttering and heavy footsteps woke Netriet in the darkness. Adrenaline rushed through her body before she was fully conscious. Fear rose up her throat and dug its fingers deep. The footfalls were coming closer. Had she been followed from the fair? Had they tracked her? She thought of Merick and his hostility toward her.

"Do you smell that?" a deep rough voice said. "There's a vampire close by."

The sound of sniffing made her cringe.

"A deserter?"

"Naw." More sniffing. "It's a female."

"Let's find her," the first voice suggested.

"What for? We need to keep moving."

"We're at war. She's the enemy."

"The war is over."

"Yeah, and we lost." The voice rumbled with rage. "I want to kill her."

The first one sighed. "Fine, just be quick about it. We need to find our party."

Netriet reached into her pack and pulled out her knife. She'd be damned if she was going to sit and wait for them to sniff her out. The shadow within her woke up at the possibility of violence and surged through the muscles of her arm. She scrambled to her feet and shot out from under the tree branches. Martia's shawl fell from her shoulders.

"There she is!" The roar came from behind her. "Get her."

Two werewolves crashed through the bracken. Netriet bobbed and weaved through the trees while they just plowed through. They were going to catch her; she wasn't fast enough.

A solid wooden ball sailed through the darkness, the moonlight dancing over the inlaid metal designs. It crashed into the back of one of the werewolves' skulls with a crunch. He fell, dead before he hit the ground. Neither Netriet nor the werewolf on her tail noticed.

"Got you!" the werewolf growled as his massive arms circled her and lifted her off the ground.

He tossed her easily in the air and caught her again so she was facing him. The moonlight highlighted his rough ugly face. His breath choked her. "I'm going to bathe in your blood." He snarled, leaned down, and licked her from collarbone to ear in one long disgusting swipe.

The darkness ran through her veins and cackled with glee. Netriet smiled. "No. I'm going to bathe in yours."

She plunged the knife clutched in her hand into his stomach. He howled and staggered back, dropping her to the ground. He ran his hand across the wound then licked the blood from his fingers. "It will take a lot more than that!"

She ducked his arm as he swung at her and stabbed him again in the side. Her blade sliced in and out six times before he connected a blow. The force of his fist sent the world spinning. The darkness retreated within and curled into a ball. She couldn't defeat him. He was too big, too rough from battle to go down with a few punctures from her little blade.

Fear returned, and she ran in a fit of terror and tears.

Another wooden ball whistled through the air, imbedding into the skull of the second werewolf, killing him as efficiently as the first.

Netriet ran blindly, believing the werewolf still chased her. Branches sliced at her skin, and she almost ran headlong into a rock wall barring her path. Her breath slammed through her lungs as she pocketed her knife and fixed her hand on the wall. She didn't care what was on the other side; she simply wanted to get in. Netriet ran around the wall, her hand skimming the surface, searching for an entrance.

Her hand shot through a thick, twisted bunch of vines. Ducking under them, Netriet found the opening. But as her body passed under the arched entry, a blinding light sliced through her eyes. A painful screaming filled her ears, and her body lifted off the ground, frozen in magic.

Chapter Nineteen

Forest dozed, her head aching and her eyes burning from crying. After the fiasco of the state dinner, and, for lack of a better term, breaking up with Syrus, Forest found she could barely lift her arms or keep a coherent thought in her head. Running home to her cottage had seemed the thing to do, but as soon as she arrived, the memories of Syrus when they were first together, there in her house, poured acid on her wound. He was everywhere. She'd held together shakily for the first few minutes after she arrived home, but when she stepped into the kitchen and saw Syrus' hair lying on the counter where she'd left it, the memory pulled her straight to the floor.

Oh, how he'd looked then. When he touched her face to know what she looked like. Her true face reflected on the surface of his eyes. She heard his voice in her head exactly as he had sounded that night. *"You're beautiful, Forest."*

"Oh, Syrus," she cried, curling into a ball on the floor. "What have I done?"

And she cried more. She cried until her eyes felt shriveled and husked with no will to pick herself up off the floor.

She dreamed she was back in the castle. *The sound of her footsteps echoed through the long hallway. She moved steadily forward to the door at the end. The heavy door swung open, and she found herself in a circular room. Seven arched passages leading off in different directions confronted her. Forest stood in the center, the urge to flee pulling at her from behind.*

Through the first passage sat Christiana's empty throne. A light breeze blew from the throne, carrying a whisper. "Choose."

Forest turned to the next passage. She saw her mother lying in the arms of Rahaxeris, and herself as a baby, cradled between them. Liasia's eyes cut right to Forest's. "Choose," she whispered.

Forest shivered and turned to the next. Scenes of the war. Soldiers, both vampires and werewolves, dying in battle. The eyes of an entire army turned and looked at her. "Choose!"

Ena stood under the next, looking down at the floor. She said nothing, just looked down.

The next passage showed Forest the council chamber of the Rune-dy. *Rahaxeris held up the necklace he'd given her. Her birthright. All of the priests turned their creepy eyes on her. "Choose," they said together.*

Forest turned to the next passage. An ache spread through her chest as she looked at Syrus standing in a circle of masters of the Blood Kata. His eyes, open and seeing, snapped to hers. "I love you."

The last doorway filled with black fabric. Billowing in the wind, falling in slow-motion. Shivers rolled though Forest as she gazed at the cloth, a bitter cold sliding under her skin. Again, it was Syrus' voice, coming through the fabric. "Good bye."

Forest turned away, wrapping her arms around her torso.

"Choose! Choose! Choose! Choose!" They all shouted at her in quick succession, their voices rising to ear-splitting shrieks.

The perimeter alarm jolted Forest from sleep. She sat up, her head pounding ruthlessly. The next second she was bolting through the house and outside. "Syrus!" she yelled, figuring blurrily it must be him. "Syrus, I'm coming."

Forest ran quickly to her key pad to stop the siren. She skidded to a halt in front of the immobilized trespasser. The immediate let down of not finding Syrus quickly gave way to shock as she recognized the woman.

"Please help me!" Netriet cried.

"You! How…how did you survive? How did you come to be here?"

Netriet looked wildly at Forest. "Please! A werewolf is after me! Please get me down!"

Forest moved forward and placed her hand through the magic that held Netriet. After a few seconds, the enchantment released her. Netriet grabbed Forest by the arm. "Are we safe? Can he get through?"

"No. He can't. Calm down. You're safe."

"Where am I?" Netriet looked around, panicked.

"It's all right. You're safe. You're safe," Forest used the same calming tone she would have used on a scared animal.

"Who are you?" Netriet demanded.

"My name's Forest. We've met before. At the lair, in Philippe's apartments. Remember?"

Netriet blinked a few times quickly. "What?"

"I looked different, I'm half shifter." It took Forest a second to remember, and then she shifted into the wonder woman look she'd used that day. "Philippe collared me," she prompted.

"Yes...I've lost a few memories since then. I remember you now. I helped you lie to Philippe. And you offered to send rescue for me...You had a vampire with you, right?"

Forest smiled. "Yes, that's right."

"Did he live?"

"Yes."

Netriet's eyebrows shot up. "You love him, whoever he is."

Forest was taken aback. "How do you know that?"

"It's obvious. You got this look around your eyes when you answered my question about him."

"Oh, well. Hmm...Why don't you come in and tell me what happened to you? You look...changed."

Netriet's shoulders sagged. "Yes. I am changed…"

She took a few steps toward the house and hesitated, her mind split and arguing. The warmth and welcome called to her. She looked at Forest and felt no threat. But her wild side clung to suspicions and thought of the knife in her pocket. Netriet tried to relax. "Do you have a mirror I could use? I'd be grateful."

"Sure. Follow me."

Netriet followed Forest into her house. Forest expected her to be shocked at the human paraphernalia, but Netriet said nothing. Instead, she scanned the living room quickly, presumably for exits.

"Your home is very nice."

"Thank you."

"What was that outside that I got caught in?" Netriet asked.

"My property was enchanted by a wizard a few years ago. There's no way around it, well, except, I suppose someone could scale the wall. It's really tall though, and I have other alarms. The noise and lights you experienced."

"Hmm. Where is your mirror, please?"

"I'll go get you one."

"No!" Netriet shot out, startling Forest. "Sorry, I just…I was hoping I could look in privacy."

Forest looked closely now at Netriet. She hadn't seen clearly the black marks on her skin or her odd swirled eye in the dark of the garden. "Jeez. What happened to you?"

Netriet trembled and looked down. "I'll tell you what I can remember, little that it is. But please let me look at myself first."

"All right," Forest said kindly. "Through that door there is a bathroom. There's a large mirror. Take your time."

Netriet closed the door behind her. It only took a minute before her sobs traveled through the door. Forest tried to ignore them, though the sound brought tears to her eyes as well. She decided to let Netriet cry herself out and not bother her.

****

Netriet looked at herself in the mirror, but it was the shadow that looked back. "I want you out of me," she whispered.

The shadow smiled wickedly and winked her dark eye.

Netriet leaned close to the mirror, examining her swirled eye. The darkness spiraled deep inside. Gasping, she pulled away from her reflection. She screamed at the shadow and slammed her fist into the mirror.

****

Forest ran, busting through the bathroom door. Netriet crouched on the floor, her fist bloody, the mirror broken.

"I'm sorry," she cried, her frame rocking back and forth. "I'll find some way to pay you back."

Forest had never seen anyone so pitiable. She crouched down and wrapped her arms around Netriet. "Don't worry about it."

Netriet laid her head against Forest's shoulder like a child. "I didn't...I didn't know...my eye. I'd seen the black scars on my arm but not the ones," she choked over the words, "not the ones on my face. I'm scary. I used to be beautiful. Now, there's... something inside me."

"What do you mean?"

"I should have died. But I woke up *different.* There's something, not me, that lives inside. It's dark. It scares me. It grabs ahold sometimes and plays me like a puppet."

Forest patted her back. "I don't have any blood here, but how about I make you some tea?"

Netriet sniffed and nodded. "All right."

Perhaps Forest should have been afraid of Netriet, unprecedented entity that she was. However, she found herself sympathetic and protective.

After Netriet ate a little, Forest ran her a bath and gave her a pair of flannel pajamas. Netriet came out of Forest's master bathroom, hair dripping, struggling to button up her shirt.

"Would you like me to help you?" Forest asked.

Netriet looked embarrassed. "Thank you."

Forest buttoned Netriet's shirt and tied a knot in the empty sleeve. "There you go."

"What were you thinking about just now?"

"Huh?"

Netriet smiled. "You got this funny look on your face. Were you remembering something?"

"Oh, yeah." Forest blushed. "It's just…something…him."

"Who is he?"

"His identity is still a secret."

"What were you remembering?" Netriet pushed.

"He asked me to help him button his shirt once. He couldn't manage it alone. He's blind."

Netriet smiled. "Couldn't manage it, eh? Sounds like a ruse to me."

"Yeah, I've often wondered if it was just so he could get his hands on me."

"Did it work?"

"Huh?"

"Did he get his hands on you then?"

"Only a little." Forest smirked. "He was laying a foundation. I'd like to hear *your* story. Would you care to sit on the couch?"

Netriet sat down and pulled her knees up to her chest. "Could I have a little more tea first?"

"Sure." Forest put the kettle back on. When she came back into the living room, Netriet was asleep. Forest covered her up with the throw and went out into her garden to watch the sunrise. Her thoughts turned to Leith as she played with the key around her neck.

Chapter Twenty

The ground under Syrus' feet vibrated ever so subtly with eons of magic. The Obsidian Mountain cast a cold shadow over him. So many years he'd wanted to be here. Never did he imagine the painful circumstances that would cloud him when he finally arrived. His heart was tight, and his chest felt bruised all around it.

He held Forest's image inside his mind. So beautiful. Too much had happened to her—she just needed time. He took a deep breath, trying to let his anger go. They would come back together. Syrus decided to try to tuck her away. He'd have no respect in the Obsidian Mountain if he showed up moping and whipped.

Since he didn't have Redge to direct him, he decided to use his magic to open his eyes, so he would at least have some sight. He focused and pulled his power from his extremities and pushed it up into his eyes. The incantation flowed from his lips, and the pressure built until his pupils felt as though they would explode. He gritted his teeth and swallowed a groan before saying the incantation again. Then came the light, disorienting and burning.

Maybe it was the influence of standing at the base of the mountain, but as Syrus' blurry sight came to him, inspiration struck, and he added a few new words to his incantation. Repeating them three times, he strengthened his weak sight, bringing more clarity and color. He innately knew the new words would also give him a longer stretch of time to see.

The entrance, ornately carved from the solid rock, stood open a few paces away, domineeringly beckoning him to enter.

"Syrus! Welcome." The pale lanky figure of a man Syrus had never seen, but knew very well, strode toward him.

Syrus smiled. "Ithiel. Thank you for having me."

Ithiel took Syrus' hands in greeting, his eyebrows rising as he looked in Syrus' eyes. "You're seeing."

"Yes, a little. It's only temporary."

"Extraordinary. You must tell me how you manage it, but first let's go in and get you settled."

Syrus followed Ithiel through the carved entrance, his eyes straining to adjust to the change in light. The cavernous room was very dark, completely bare, and surprisingly beautiful. Light streamed in through random patches of black volcanic glass, giving the space the feeling of a cathedral.

"We keep a room for opening portals, if you ever need to leave quickly." Ithiel pointed to a plain door on the far wall. "It's guarded by our resident ogre, Len."

He led Syrus up a long stretch of stairs roughly cut from the rock. It seemed to take forever to get anywhere. The stairs wound around the edge. Occasionally passages branched off, but Ithiel ignored them and continued upward. Finally, they emerged into another cavernous room. The ceiling was domed, a black fire burned continuously in the center, and one side of the room opened to the sky. Syrus stepped slowly toward the open wall, not daring to get too close in case his eyes misjudged. It was like a huge balcony without a safety rail. He could simply step off the edge and fall to his death.

"Odd," Syrus said gesturing to the edge.

"Only the best and some might argue the stupidest, spar in here. I use this arena to teach the value of physical awareness in battle. Care to try it?"

Syrus laughed. "Not until my sight is gone. When I'm fully blind this will be no problem."

"Still full of bravado, I see. But I feel your emotions rule you."

Syrus blew out a breath and crossed his arms. Damn, if Ithiel didn't have him there. "It's a matter of circumstances."

"Isn't it always?"

"I thought coming here would help me regain control, but if that reason seems insufficient, or base, I'll leave."

Ithiel waved his hand dismissively. "Don't be absurd. Why do you think most come here? Besides, I'm honored to have you. You have more right than me to be here. I'm not even a mage. In fact, you are the only mage to set foot here in a hundred years."

"Really?"

"Yes, indeed. The others are going to be so excited."

"Where are the others?" Syrus asked.

"Most are still away because of the war. I've only two tyro masters here now, and they are currently in the middle of their isolation."

"So you're the only company I can expect for the next few days?"

Ithiel smirked. "Disappointing, I know. Come on, I'll show you to your apartments."

"There's the issue of my name and the fact that I'm still technically dead. How are you going to introduce me to the other masters?"

"I'll tell them you are The Sanguine Mage, which you are, and that they are to address you as sir. Does that suit you?"

"Yes, for now."

Syrus' apartments were far from glamorous. Nothing short of what he'd expected, and he found the simplicity comforting. A sleeping mat flat on the floor, a small rock fire pit, and a roughhewn window.

He stood at his window, watching the sky, waiting to see how long his sight would last.

****

A storm brewed under the surface in the Onyx Castle. Despite the smiles and courtesy, Zeren announcing his adoption of an unknown Halfling as his heir had shocked, insulted, and enraged the aristocracy. Treasonous whispers rippled through the halls. The discovery of Lorcan's body had added to the outrage but laced it with a heavy dose of fear. No one had seen Rahaxeris, but that fact alone didn't inspire enough confidence to bring about action. Those who had come in contact with Rahaxeris believed he could see and hear everything.

Dracula had as healthy a fear as anyone of Rahaxeris, but he also had more arrogance. What Zeren did had deeply offended his sensibilities. But the murder of his nephew's son was the limit of what he could take. He began gleaning every stray bit of hushed gossip floating around the castle. Plenty of it was sensationalized tripe, but one tip led him to find Leith's cell. He watched it secretly for two days. The door was guarded around the clock by an ogre, switching in shifts once a day.

Dracula didn't know for sure that it was Leith behind the door, yet he'd seen the deadly intent in Rahaxeris' eyes when he'd arrested him. But Rahaxeris was nowhere to be found. Dracula sent word to Leith's father, Vladien, to come to the castle as soon as possible and meet him at the servants' entrance after midnight.

After all of the servants had left to relax or go off to sleep, he waited. Vladien arrived promptly a few minutes after midnight, his white-blond head shrouded in a hood. They silently acknowledged each other, and Dracula led him to an empty storeroom. Vladien pulled his hood back, and the traces of grief pulled across his face.

"I'm sorry for your loss," Dracula said bracingly. "Lorcan was an exceptional young man."

Vladien's mouth turned into a thin line, and he nodded, looking down. "You think you know where Leith is?"

"I think so. I'm almost sure of it."

The light of desperation shone in Vladien's eyes.

Dracula placed a hand on his shoulder. "There is an obstacle. He's being guarded."

"One or two ogres are no problem."

"It's not just that. Leith was put under arrest by Rahaxeris himself. I saw it with my own eyes. And I'll be a werewolf if that *Rune-dy* didn't have something personal against him. So, I'd bet there's more than just one ogre holding him there."

Vladien's eyes slid out of focus. "I have an idea. But I need your help. We might need a few others as well. Are you in or out?"

****

Merhl leaned against the wall, his mind drifting, imagining faraway lands. His hands throbbed painfully. He was quite sure he was the only one in the castle who was looking forward to Rahaxeris' return. He needed something to do other than guard this infernal door.

Goosebumps on the back of his neck pulled him from his reverie, two seconds before the commotion landed at his feet.

"Open the door, ogre! Open it now, or I'll kill him!"

Merhl blinked in shock. Two vampires he knew now faced him. Vladien held Dracula from behind, a long blade to his throat. Both vampires looked crazed—Vladien with desperation and Dracula with fear. Merhl had heard about Lorcan's death and understood Vladien was capable of anything. For one second, one long agonizing second, Merhl hesitated. He had pledged allegiance to Rahaxeris. But protecting the lives of vampires was in his nature, and if Dracula died because of him, his life would be forfeit as well.

"Open it now!" Vladien shouted again, cutting a small line on Dracula's neck.

Merhl turned to the door, breaking the magic he put in place. The hilt of Vladien's dagger came down sharply on the back of his head, sending him to the floor.

****

"Damn it, you didn't have to really cut me," Dracula complained as Vladien kicked in the door to Leith's cell.

Vladien grabbed Leith and threw him over his shoulder before charging back out. "Let's go!" he growled at Dracula.

"I'm not going with you, fool. How would that look? Take the door on the right at the end. Sharpe will have cleared the side exit of anyone by now. You should have a straight shot if you go now."

Vladien nodded quickly and charged off down the dark hallway, Leith hanging over his shoulder like a rag doll.

Dracula roughed up his hair, smeared some of the blood from the little cut on his neck onto his face, and laid down next to Merhl as though he too had been knocked out, and waited for the ogre to wake up or someone else to stumble over them and raise the alarm.

Chapter Twenty-one

Forest tried to wake Netriet the next morning to no avail. She checked her vital signs. She seemed healthy enough. She shook her roughly, pinched her arm—nothing roused her. So Forest picked her up, carted her into the spare bedroom, and tucked her in the bed. Netriet seemed so unstable, Forest thought it best to stay close, so she didn't wake up alone.

Netriet didn't budge for two days.

Forest occupied herself with cleaning, gardening, organizing her basement, and packing a large bag of stuff for Tek. She was overly generous with the earthly goods she packed reminding herself that she hadn't restocked him in quite a while, and since the portals were shut none of her competitors would have much if anything to offer.

 Her thoughts were so muddy and her emotions so up and down, she wasn't sure if she'd had any moments of clarity or not. She dreamed of Syrus at night and woke up with tears soaking the pillow. The pain of not being together was not the insanity she'd suffered when she'd been banished. Perhaps it wasn't so acute because they were both in Regia and not separated by galaxies. But still, her heart twisted and tore. Her pride kept her from running to him, and she assumed his pride kept him from doing the same.

Forest went back into her basement to get the last of the old magazines for the package for Tek. When she came back up, Netriet was sitting calmly on the couch.

"Hello."

"I'm glad you're finally awake. I was getting worried."

"How long was I out?"

"Almost three days. I didn't know a vampire could sleep that long."

Netriet picked absently at her empty sleeve. "I've been traveling for a long time, never feeling quite safe enough to really sleep...I feel much better. I'll get myself together and be out of your way as soon as I can."

"You don't have to rush. Are you planning to go back to Halussis?"

"Since I woke up, after not dying, I've thought about going home. But every time I think about it seriously, I know I can't go back. Not like this. I wouldn't be...treated well."

"But you killed Philippe, didn't you?"

Netriet nodded dismissively.

"You're a hero to your people."

"No. They wouldn't treat me like that. I'm a convict, with a death sentence. And they'd look at me and see nothing but that I'd been tainted by a wolf."

Forest sat down across from Netriet. "Please tell me everything that happened to you."

Netriet laughed humorlessly. "Why should I?"

"Because maybe I can help you."

Netriet eyed Forest with speculation. "You've been kind to me...If I was going to trust anyone, I guess it should be you. Where should I start?"

"Start with your crime."

Netriet leaned back on the couch. "All right. I'll tell you everything I can remember. You'll have to forgive me the rest."

Forest listened, amazed at what she learned and frustrated by what Netriet couldn't remember. She looked at Netriet's empty sleeve when she recounted the torture she'd suffered at Philippe's hand, and shivered as she remembered what it had been like to wear the collar. She was not only thankful to still be alive, but that she still had both arms.

When Netriet told her about the transparent being that saved her life, Forest bit down on her tongue. The hateful glint in Netriet's eyes stopped her from saying anything at all about Shi.

"I suppose whatever it was that saved my life meant well, but the cost..." Netriet shuddered. "The cost is too high. I would have preferred to die."

She finished her tale by recounting the places and people she'd encountered from the Wolf's Wood down to Forest's garden gate.

"So, how do *you* think you can help me?" Netriet asked snidely. "You, a Halfling, who lives like an outcast?"

Forest laughed a little and then she laughed harder, until tears of mirth were rolling down her cheeks. "Yes, an outcast Halfling. That used to be me, but I know people." She chortled. "I've got friends in high places, hell, *I'm* in high places."

Netriet's look of incredulity sobered Forest a little. "I'm Zeren's adopted daughter."

Netriet snorted. "The hell you are. You're even crazier than me."

Forest chuckled again and shook her head. "And that's small beans compared to who my real father is...I think it's time I tell you my story. I'm going to get us some tea. This could take a while. If you're willing to hear it, I'd like to tell you the whole thing. You're the first person I've wanted to tell it to, and I think maybe you hearing it could help me."

"What do you mean the *whole* thing?" Netriet asked as Forest went to the kitchen.

"I mean the whole thing, starting with how I came to be alive."

"Well, hell," Netriet took a deep sigh. "I guess I owe you for lodging. All right I'll listen to you, crazy woman."

Forest told Netriet everything. Everything about Leith, her father, her childhood- omitting her relationship with Shi, and her past illegal activities. When she came to the part of her story where she took the mission to protect Syrus, she threw caution to the wind and told her exactly whom she was protecting. Despite her initial grumblings, Netriet's attention wrapped around Forest's every word.

"...So now, he's hurting, and I'm hurting. I can't stomach the idea of being the queen and I just don't know what to do. But the longer I hesitate, the worse it is for the people. I know everyone is waiting for something to make sense again in Regia, and I feel like the whole damn thing rests on my shoulders."

Netriet heaved a deep sigh. "Are you sure you want to know what I think?"

"Yes," Forest said desperately.

"You're an idiot. A great bumbling idiot. I'd kick your ass, if I could, for being so stupid."

Forest gaped at Netriet.

"Whole worlds do not rest on one person's shoulders. If that were true, you'd have been forced into a position long before now, and there wouldn't be a darn thing you could do about it. But as it is, there are three, *three* very powerful men who have stepped back and told you to figure out what *you* want. Yet, here you sit, whining that you don't know!

"You made it plain, in what you told me of your life, that you always wanted to have an influence for good. You've been kicked around, and you want to stand up for other's who are kicked around. Am I right?"

"Yes. Exactly. When I worked for Fortress, it was my dream to one day become a council member. To represent those who were not represented. But I knew it would never happen."

"Wake up," Netriet said sharply. "Why won't you take the position your father offers you?"

Forest stood up and paced the room. "Because I didn't earn it!" she fired back. "I don't want to be given anything. It's weak."

"Oh, *waaa*. All of us have to take what we're given and use it. Syrus is the prince. He didn't earn that. Is he weak?"

"No," Forest said slowly.

"Look, Forest, I think you're pretty awesome."

Forest snorted and rolled her eyes.

"No, really," Netriet pressed. "You're an amazing person. You're just an ingrate."

Forest stopped pacing and stared at Netriet. The word *ingrate* caught her sideways.

"You've had a bum deal, I'll admit it. And it's gotten to your head. You've been handed the job of your dreams, and you spit on it. You've been given respect and position, and you act like a guttersnipe. And you've got Syrus! Jeez, *Syrus!* And you hurt him and send him away. More than a few other women would be happy to swoop in and comfort him, myself included. But he's yours, forever, without question, because he's your destined life mate. He'll never love anyone but you. Why do you reject it?"

Forest sank back onto the chair, her head in her hands. "I don't know...I don't know."

"Yes, you do," Netriet insisted.

Forest's head shot up. "I don't deserve him."

"Says who? Did Syrus say that?"

"No."

"You've got to kill Leith as soon as possible."

Forest looked away. Netriet watched her closely as she stood up and paced again.

"Wow," Netriet said slowly, "There's something really twisted in your head isn't there?"

"Yes," Forest whispered. "When Leith picked me, despite the brutality, and the hate, a part of me felt like he had honored me."

Netriet rushed at Forest and cracked a vicious slap across her face before she could react. Her handprint glowed on Forest's cheek. She didn't attack or fight back in any way. Forest pressed a hand to her throbbing face for a moment before pulling Netriet into a tight hug.

"Thanks. I needed that," Forest said earnestly.

"You surely did."

Forest released Netriet and rushed to her bedroom. "I've got to go," she said, grabbing an empty duffle bag from her closet and filling it with a few days' clothes.

Ten minutes later Forest stood at her front door, strapping on her sword and stuffing the Hailemarris amulet in her pocket. "You're welcome to stay here as long as you need to, Netriet. You'll be perfectly safe."

"Thanks," Netriet said. "I appreciate it. Now go, and good luck to you."

****

Netriet sat quietly after Forest left, thinking about her. She considered her a friend, but the nice feelings she harbored began to get pushed to the back as the shadow came crawling out. A surge of jealousy rocked through her. Forest was beautiful, more beautiful then she had been before Philippe got a hold of her. She had power, a rising position, and love. Mordant coated Netriet's insides as she thought of Syrus.

Netriet had mourned him terribly when she learned he was dead. The memory of the first time she'd ever laid eyes on Syrus swam in her mind. When she was barely more than a girl, Syrus had looked at her and smiled and that was all she needed. All throughout her adolescence, her heart was lost to Syrus as she served Christiana.

Yes! The shadow hissed. *You hate her. She's stolen something from you.*

"No. She's my friend," Netriet said aloud.

You have no friends but me. I'm your only friend. She's the one who ruined your happiness. Stole it. The happiness that should be ours. Syrus should be ours.

Netriet shook her head, wishing she could stop her ears to the shadow.

We should leave, but not before you steal from her. Break her precious little house to bits. Steal her beloved possessions.

Tears ran down Netriet's cheeks. The jealousy was real, and the shadow would continue to plague her if she stayed. With a heavy heart and bitterness blackening her mind, Netriet put her dirty clothes back on and left Forest's house before she did something she regretted.

She looked back at Forest's rock wall as she left. The trees reached out to her like the twisted arms of demon lovers. She thought about the people she'd met at the fair. They were too nice for her. If she went there, she'd hurt them. No, the wild was better.

She walked northeast for a quarter mile before coming to a sudden cliff. The ground in front of her dropped straight down to jagged rocks below. The thought to jump came to her mind, but the shadow quickly shoved her back from the edge. She walked away, accepting the nasty truth that she would survive a long time. The darkness within had too strong a will to live.

****

Syrus sat in deep mediation in the center of the sparing arena. Ithiel was doing everything in his power, short of physical harm, to break his concentration. Ithiel's attempts weren't even close to scratching the surface. Syrus rolled in the depths of his subconscious, journeying further in. The sorrow surrounding Forest aside, he had never felt happier. Everything inside him clicked into place in the Obsidian Mountain. It was where he belonged. Training the new masters was the work he was meant for.

He pulled back from mediation as his heart gave a little shiver.

He opened his blurry eyes to see both Guyas and Taurus, the newbie mages, standing in front of him, practically bouncing on their toes, with silly grins on their faces. Syrus said his revised incantation once under his breath, strengthening his sight.

He quirked an eyebrow. *"What?"*

"You've got a visitor, sir," Guyas said.

"Waiting in your apartment, sir," Taurus added.

Syrus stood and brushed past them, glancing once over his shoulder at Ithiel, who also had a silly grin on his face. The shiver continued as Syrus climbed the stairs to his room.

She had her back to him, looking out the window. Syrus closed his eyelids and said his incantation a few more times under his breath, so she couldn't hear. He kept his eyes shut as she turned to face him.

The pain and anger stood in the room between them like another person. Her heart spoke remorse and apology to his, but no words were uttered. The bond trembled and pulled at them. Syrus didn't move when she took a tentative step toward him. His face remained closed with anger.

Forest watched him warily as she took another step closer. A muscle in his jaw tightened. It seemed as though she hadn't looked at him in years, and she realized clearly that she had never seen a more beautiful man. Angry or not, she wanted to touch him, to press her lips to his skin, to lay her head on his strong chest and be wrapped in his arms.

Absorbing her release of pheromones, the anger in Syrus' face shifted to a bemused curiosity. The corner of his mouth turned up, and he opened his eyes. She gasped at the one-two punch to her head and heart at the eye contact. He reached out and grabbed her by the arm, pulling her roughly against him.

Relief and pleasure flooded through her at his touch.

For a long time, they just stood there, silently holding on to each other. When she pressed a kiss on his collarbone, he pulled back and looked in her eyes again. "I'm angry still," he said.

"Forgive me."

He sighed. "I will, just not today."

Forest looked down at the floor, dejected. She lifted her hair off one shoulder and pressed back against him. Tilting her head, offering him her neck.

He stiffened. "No." He pushed away from her. "I'm too angry. I'd hurt you."

Syrus threw his hands up at her sad, wide-eyed expression. "Well I'm not made of stone," he said exasperated.

"I just came here to tell you that I love you, and I'm sorry. I stopped here on my way to Kyhael."

"Kyhael?"

"Yes. I'm going to see my father and accept my birthright. Unless you don't approve. I intend to become Hailemarris."

It had been too long since Forest had seen Syrus' childlike smile and it shone on her now like the sunlight. He caught her hand in his and kissed it. "That's good. I'm happy you've decided. I think it's the right choice for you."

"And what about you?"

"I'm figuring it out. Things are more clear for me here, on the mountain."

"They are?"

He smirked. "Everything except you. Troublesome little addiction that you are."

"I'm sorry."

"Sure you are," he said sarcastically.

To her great relief, Syrus reached for her again and kissed her mouth without holding back. She melted and strained against him, pushing his cloak off his shoulders. Her hands running down his arms and over the planes of his back teased out shivers on his skin.

Desperately tormented, he grabbed the hem of her shirt and pulled it over her head. He lifted her off her feet, holding her against him, heart to heart. Trailing kisses from her mouth to her jaw and down her neck where his lips touched her slave mark, dousing his fire as effectively as a bucket of cold water. He sighed and placed her back on her feet. "We're not whole yet," he said sadly. "How much longer are you going to make me wait?"

"As soon as I am Hailemarris, I'll go back to the Onyx Castle and kill Leith."

He kissed her once more, abruptly. "I love you, Forest."

"I love you, Syrus." She retrieved her shirt off the floor and put it back on. "Not much longer, love. Not much longer."

"All right. I'll be here."

"Thank you."

"For what?"

"Forgiveness." She lifted his hand and placed it over her heart. "Listen to it while we're apart."

"I do, always." He placed her hand over his heart. "You need to get better at listening to mine."

"You're right. I'll do better."

The ogre, Len, was more than happy to open a portal for her to the gate of Kyhael. Forest was both optimistic and heavyhearted when she left Syrus. Looking forward at her future career and their future together, she moved ahead, unaware of the danger lurking in the shadows.

Chapter Twenty-two

Devonte yawned and rolled his shoulders before checking Leith's progress again. The surgery to remove the black thorns had been rough, and he was healing slowly. The incisions were in danger of infection and would create ugly scars regardless of what Devonte did.

Vladien came into the dark room and looked down at his son, thrashing in his fevered sleep. "What do you think, Devonte?"

"He'll live. You were right to send for me."

Vladien's head boiled. He wouldn't stand for this. He wouldn't sit quietly while his race decided they were no longer superior. And he wouldn't let anyone, regardless of their rank or title, pass judgment on his son.

Sudden grief for Lorcan seized in his throat, and he excused himself from the room. Holding up in this non-descript house in the low-class end of Paradigm was necessary while Leith was wanted. The bodies of the previous owners still lay in their beds.

"Vladien," Devonte called, "he's waking."

Vladien rushed back into the other room and knelt down next to his son. Beads of sweat covered Leith's skin, and his eyes fluttered. He moaned and murmured.

Leith sprang into a sitting position, grabbing his father by the arm, his bloodshot eyes wild and unfocused. "Forest! Where is she?"

Vladien pushed Leith back. His muscles convulsed a few times before he slipped back into unconsciousness. Vladien stood and straightened his shirtfront, sneering down at his son. "Idiot, boy," he snarled and then looked at Devonte. "We need to talk."

The hunched wizard followed Vladien into the next room. Vladien paced the length of the floor a few times before turning his icy eyes on Devonte. "That Halfling is the cause of all of this! She killed Lorcan."

"Sir, Forest was at the ball when Lorcan was killed."

"She killed him, do you hear me?"

Devonte shrugged, unperturbed. "Calm yourself, or I'll leave."

"You'll do as I say!"

"I don't answer to you. I came because I sympathize with your plight. Don't push me."

"I want her dead. She's trouble. You can take her out."

Devonte scratched his nose as though bored. "I don't give a damn about her one way or the other. And I've had enough of your drama. If she's such a bother to Leith, let him take care of it. He'll be back on his feet in a few days."

Vladien offered no thanks or acknowledgment of any kind to Devonte when he left, except to slam the door behind him.

Devonte contemplated reporting their location once he returned to Fortress out of annoyance at how he'd been treated, but on second thought, he really didn't want to draw attention to himself at the moment. His thoughts shifted to a good meal and a nap.

****

The portal from the Obsidian Mountain dropped Forest directly in front of Kyhael's main gate. The gate stood wide open, deceptively welcoming. Forest gulped and took a step back, her heart beating painfully fast. Never had she dared to venture this close to the elf city before. The light radiating from the Belliss stone was warm, golden, and alabaster, its luminescence coming from within and not a reflection of the pale sun.

The urge to run slammed through her feet. Her thoughts were a mess. She tried to create a cover story and a lie about her business and identity, as she knew she would be questioned as soon as she entered. Then she took a deep breath and shook her head, laughing to herself. She didn't need a cover story or a fake name. She didn't come here to hide, but be recognized. The sensation was completely new.

Forest wiped her sweaty palms on her jeans and did a quick appearance check. She was still in her wonder woman mode. Remembering what Rahaxeris said about choosing an appearance that people could recognize her with, she shifted back into the look that closely resembled her true form, tucking her hair behind her ears, so everyone could see she was an elf.

She lifted her chin, walked through the gate, and was immediately stopped by two armed guards. Both of them smiled vaguely in an attempt to seem cordial while emanating the sense they would take her down in the blink of an eye, if need be. They resembled each other so closely they could have been twins. Forest admired the official white-handled swords that hung from their belts.

"A few questions, please, citizen."

"Citizen?" Forest asked.

"All elves have citizenship in Kyhael. Is this your first time to the city?"

"Yes. It is."

The guards glanced at each other for a second. "Are you here on business or pleasure?"

"Umm. Some of both, actually."

Their eyes grew more intense. "You are not a full-blood elf," the one on her right said sternly.

The ingrained urge to look down pulled at her. Forest fought it, keeping her chin up. "That's right. I'm half shifter."

The guards glanced at each other again, some significant communication passing between them silently. "State your name, please, citizen."

"I am the Lady Forest. Zeren's adopted daughter and I'm here to see the *Rune-dy*."

Within three minutes, Forest was surrounded by Kyhael officials, all wanting to escort her to the *Rune-dy*. They fussed and tripped over themselves offering her warm welcomes and any comfort she might desire. People on the street stopped, stared, and moved aside for her and the entourage around her.

Their words faded into a buzzing in the background as Forest beheld the full beauty of the elf city for the first time in her life. The streets, walls, and buildings all seemed to flow from the Belliss stone rather than have been cut from it. Nothing was stacked, or rough-edged. The entire city was seamless, a shining example of balance and harmony.

****

Rahaxeris looked up from the report he was reading. Forest was close by; he could feel her. Surprised she would just show up and pleased she possessed the courage to do so, Rahaxeris got up to see which of his fellow priests were at work and inform them of her arrival.

After looking through every room, he found he was alone except for Baal, who was doing paperwork in the science library.

"Baal," Rahaxeris addressed the assistant.

Baal jumped to his feet. "Yes, sir."

"Forest is coming in, in a few minutes, and I'd like to speak to her privately."

Baal folded his notes and tucked them under his arm. "Yes, sir...I didn't know she was coming today."

Rahaxeris smiled. "Neither did I, otherwise I'd have informed everyone."

Baal hesitated at the door. "May I meet her, sir? Just briefly?"

Rahaxeris raised one eyebrow. "Scientific curiosity?"

"Yes, sir."

"*Very* briefly."

The *Rune-dy's* upper office was located in the dead center of Kyhael. Forest found she didn't have to speak for herself as the officials all started barking orders at the office staff. She looked around at the efficient simplicity, feeling a chill run up her spine as she reminded herself of the atrocities that were committed behind the walls.

"I shall escort the Lady from here. Thank you for bringing her in, but please leave now."

Forest surveyed the elf ushering the officials out before he turned to smile at her. "I am the prefect Camber." He took her hand in a welcoming gesture. "You honor us with your presence."

Forest made a non-committal noise in her throat. She pegged Camber immediately as the perfect lackey. Useful, but she didn't like him at all.

"If there is anything, anything at all that I can get for you, please don't hesitate to ask."

His smile fell a fraction when she made no request of him or gave him thanks like a treat to an anxious, performing dog.

"Please follow me."

As Forest followed Camber down the narrow tunnels, she fought the urge to turn and run back to the surface. Her mind conjured all manner of horrors that might lie below. Once her imagination kicked in, cold dread swirled in her stomach. The *Rune-dy* might still strap her to a table and dissect her for answers.

Everything Rahaxeris said might have been a ruse, in an attempt to lure her here.

Syrus' logical words came back into her mind. If Rahaxeris wanted her, she wouldn't have been able to hide from him. He didn't need to deceive to get her.

She came to a halt behind Camber in front of a curved wall, a circle of light shone through the center, no bigger than Camber's palm. He placed his hand over it, and the light expanded until it was taller and wider than the two of them. He stepped back. "After you."

"I don't think so," she said sternly.

He smiled and gave her a little bow. "As you wish." He walked through the light.

Forest's pulse hammered, and she blew out her breath. *Okay, here goes.* She stepped into the light and passed right through the wall.

Rahaxeris waited on the other side. She met his red-eyed gaze evenly. *Father.* Her mind rolled with the word, again finding it odd, but not rejecting it.

He turned a smile on Camber. "Thank you, Camber. You may leave."

"Yes, Sir."

Rahaxeris looked at her silently until the light closed behind Camber.

"So, Forest. What brings you here?"

She reached into her pocket, pulled the green stone necklace out, and held it up.

A stony expression hardened on his face. "Did you come all this way just to give it back?"

"No. You're mistaken. I came here to accept it and claim my birthright."

Pleasure flashed through his eyes, and he quickly worked to neutralize it. "Well, I am...pleased."

Forest chuckled then sobered. "I'm not doing it to please you. I'm taking the job so I can do good. So I can speak for those who have no voice, as I myself was once silent...And though some will judge me to be a monster once they learn whose child I am, I find that I long to have a surname."

At Rahaxeris' quick smile, she rushed to clarify. "Accepting my title puts me on more even ground with Syrus. I want to be considered his equal. It's vital to my future happiness."

Her statement didn't dampen his smile. "I'm happy my name will contribute to your future happiness, Forest...I know that my knowledge about you, irks you, but I think you'll find it agreeable when I tell you that the position of Hailemarris is not absolute or forever."

"Huh?"

"I know you like to earn what you have. You shall be instated as Hailemarris, but after five years, as the new republic finds its feet, you will only be able to keep your position by a majority vote of the people."

Forest's mouth fell open. "Really?"

"Really."

"Thank you." It was the first genuine smile she'd given him, and his heart absorbed it. She slipped the necklace over her head, the power sliding over her skin, filling her pores like smoke. "So, what do we do now?"

"I'll send word to Zefyre, telling her of your decision, and to be expecting my official letter to the high council. Then one to Zeren. Trust me, word will spread quickly. Do you need to notify anyone?"

"No. I told Syrus before I came here. Will I be an employee of Fortress again?"

Rahaxeris chuckled. "Hardly. More like the boss. I've already had your office constructed in Fortress castle, but if you'd prefer to be in another location, it can be arranged easily."

Forest considered. "I suppose it will be best that I am there, given the nature of the job, and the central location…I'm sure the members of the high council will dislike the change."

"You have the ability to terminate the job of anyone who works for Fortress, including the members of the high council…in fact, I think you'll find your plate full, very quickly, with charges brought against a few you know."

"What?"

"Zefyre and Lush must come under your judgment, soon. Frost and Gagnee face lesser charges. And then there's Devonte…The lawless actions of the wizards will no longer be met with acceptance. They will obey the laws or face banishment back to their homeland."

Forest swallowed and took a deep breath. "Damn. No honeymoon period then."

Rahaxeris' stare bored into her. "You're perfect for this job, Forest. I have no doubt."

His confidence was solid and real. She could stand on it. "Thank you…Father."

"Would you like to see what we do down here?"

Trepidation crept into Forest's muscles as she looked over Rahaxeris' shoulder. He noticed.

"If you're not comfortable…"

Her gaze cut to his. "I most certainly am *not* comfortable. But the choice of ignorance is for cowards. Show me."

"Very well."

Ice crystallized down Forest's vertebrae as she followed. He brought her into a library first, where another priest sat reading. He looked up at them, quickly closed his book, and stood.

"Forest, this is Baal. He's an assistant."

Baal inclined his head.

"Nice to meet you," Forest said.

Baal was dressed like Rahaxeris, though a bit plainer. His eyes were also red, and his black hair hung board-straight to his shoulders. His appearance wasn't anywhere near as frightening as Rahaxeris', but he still put her system on alert. Dangerous, but on a lesser level than her father.

"I'm happy to finally meet you in person, Forest. You have fascinated me for a long time...I see you have accepted the title. I look forward to working with you in the future."

"Uh, thank you."

"Baal will go with you when you leave here," Rahaxeris said. "Assuming that you are heading straight to Fortress."

"Oh, well...okay. I guess that would be better than you going with me?"

"I didn't want it to look like daddy taking his little girl to school."

"Ah, yes." Forest managed a small smile. "We can't have that."

"So, anyway, this is the science library. Self-explanatory. Come on."

Forest nodded to Baal, who nodded back and resumed his seat as they left the room. She followed past a basic meeting room, and then into the science lab. She looked at the odd jars lining the walls before approaching the table in the center of the room, diagrams and charts covered the surface. Forest looked down at the papers, understanding less than half of what she saw. The word *unsuccessful* was written harshly across the top of the paper. It stuck a chord and she turned to face her father. "I want to see the files from the experiment that spawned me."

Rahaxeris crossed his arms. "Just because you are here doesn't mean I can show you anything you want to see. You don't have clearance for that."

"You could give me clearance," Forest fired back.

"Perhaps I could, but I won't."

Forest hissed out an angry breath. "Why? Because it's so ugly?"

"Yes."

The tears rising in Forest's eyes surprised her. She wrapped her arms around her middle, thinking of the ones who had been created then deemed *unsuccessful* and destroyed. She turned her back to him, letting the tears fall down her cheeks, mourning them as siblings.

 Rahaxeris came up behind her and put his sharp hand on her arm. "Come with me. I need to show you something else."

Forest let him lead her by the arm out of the room and into another. She dug in her heels as she crossed the threshold. It was an operating theater, empty, sanitized, and completely haunted by the tortured dead.

"Yes, you see. And you know the rumors. But what we do is for the greater good."

Forest looked at him helplessly.

"You believe in the greater good, don't you?" he asked gently.

She nodded. "Yes."

"You understand the usefulness of fear?"

"Yes."

"Fear of punishment keeps people safe, safe from others, and from the evil within themselves. So, just as we cultivate fear, and contrive pain for punishment, we create balance and peace. It's not a job just anyone can do."

Forest stared at the operating table and shivered. "That's for damn sure."

"And with science, experimentation must be detached. But through probing for answers we have learned, many ways to heal, improve life, and prolong it. Death happens in the process."

Forest looked back into his eyes shaking her head. "I've seen enough."

"No, I don't think you have. Come on."

Rahaxeris led her back to a plain room, the stone opening and sealing again behind her. The room was empty. "These are my personal quarters. I want to show you my memories."

"Your memories?"

"Unless you don't want to."

"I'd be lying if I said I wasn't intrigued."

"All right."

Rahaxeris placed his palm flat on the wall, closing his eyes and muttering a few words under his breath. A grey fog rose off the stone around his hand, quickly filling the room, drifting over the floor like a haze in a swamp. The ghostly image of a woman gathered from the mist and stood in front of Forest. She jumped back, her mouth falling open as she recognized her mother. Liasia never was one to shift her appearance too much. She stuck to five different looks. What Forest saw was a face she knew well. Her mother looked at her silently as other transparent people formed around her, joining her in a line.

Liasia looked down at a parchment in her hands as the line moved. She looked up again, her eyes fixing across the room, her mouth falling open slightly. Forest followed her gaze and saw a ghostly version of her father standing next to her real father. Ghostly Rahaxeris looked as trapped and transfixed as Liasia. Forest realized she'd just witnessed the first time her parents laid eyes on each other.

The images melted back into the haze, replaced by new ones. Forest blushed at seeing her parents lying in each other's arms in a room she recognized as her mother's. Liasia nestled her head onto Rahaxeris' bare shoulder. *I love you*, she whispered.

I'll take care of you, Lia.

The haze again shifted. Liasia was crying uncontrollably against Rahaxeris' chest. *He took her, Ra! That bastard, Menjel, took our baby!*

I'll get her back, I promise.

Forest's heart clenched at the sound of her mother's anguished sobs, grateful when the haze changed again. Rahaxeris was in a shouting match with another priest, whom she assumed was Menjel.

She's shown us everything we need to know. Her life has fulfilled its purpose.

You don't know that she's shown us everything! Rahaxeris yelled. *Many elves cannot master invisibility until puberty. Let's see what she can do as she gets older. No other splice came out as good as she did.*

Ah, yes, well she's not really even a splice is she? She's just a Halfling bastard.

I won't let you kill her! Her mother loves her.

What is that to me? Or the project? Menjel argued.

I promised Liasia she could raise her child.

You weren't given that kind of authority.

It's MY project. And she's my daughter. I want to see what she can do as she grows up.

The haze shifted again. Rahaxeris looked down at Forest as a baby, sleeping in his arms. He was in the room she grew up in, sitting in a rocking chair. He stroked the side of her baby face and played with the wispy strands of hair on her head. Forest was nonplused at the simple show of affection.

The haze shifted back to her parents.

I can't keep coming back. If they found out, it would put her life in danger.

What do I tell her about you? As she gets older?

Nothing. She's safer that way. She won't lack for anything, Lia. I promise.

Her mother turned away, her face in her hands. *Don't make me anymore promises, Ra. Just keep the only one that matters and let me raise her to adulthood.*

The images then shifted so quickly it was as if he was fast-forwarding. And indeed, when it slowed down, time had jumped from her being a baby to around the time Leith first targeted her. Rahaxeris was arguing again with Menjel. Other priests gathered around them.

I can't let her suffer like that! It's unjust. He's broken Regia's slave laws.

You argued before that we should leave her alone and see what she does. I think now is the perfect time to do just that, Menjel reasoned coldly.

We did all agree not to interfere, Rahaxeris, another added.

The haze shifted for the last time. Rahaxeris sat next to her mother's deathbed, holding her hand.

She's not coping well, Ra, Lia rasped.

I've been working hard to become the next High Priest. It won't be much longer. I'll fix it for her, Lia. I'll fix the whole damn world.

Then let that be the last promise you make me. Promise me, now as I'm dying. Promise you won't fail her.

Rahaxeris brought Liasia's hand to his lips. *I promise.*

All the haze in the room evaporated, leaving Forest gaping at her father.

"I love you, Forest... I'm trying to fulfill my promise."

A grievous crack snaked up from the foundation through the walls of Forest's defenses, and she found herself running into her father's arms. Strange, frightening being that he was, he held her as any loving father would and absorbed the rocking waves of her tears.

I am wanted. I know who I am and where I came from. I matter. And I am loved.

The knowledge brought nourishment to her bruised and battered heart. All the scars vanished away. All the scars but one...Leith's.

Forest's slave mark now prickled and strung. It had to go, right now. Pride radiated through her. She was Forest, daughter of Rahaxeris, and no man's slave.

She wiped her eyes and lifted her chin. "I have to get back to the Onyx Castle, now. I have unfinished business that cannot wait another day."

"About time. I'll send you back there directly."

"You can create portals, too?"

"Forest, you have no idea the amount of things I can do." He smiled at her and struck the air. The portal swirled before her.

"Will you teach me to do some of the things you can?"

He shook his head ruefully. "My knowledge has come from dozens of decades of experimenting and dabbling. Trust me, the cost is high. Your soul is too important."

"I would have to forfeit my soul to gain what you have?"

"I'm afraid so."

"Then I think I'm content the way I am."

"A wise choice. I'll send Baal to Fortress. He'll be there to help you after you've handled your unfinished business in the Onyx Castle. Don't be afraid to boss Baal around a bit. He'll be there to help you. Just boss him respectfully."

"Sure, no problem." She stepped toward the portal and turned back to him. "Thank you, Father."

He nodded a little stiffly, and then he and his room disappeared in the rushing blackness as she sped back to the castle.

The portal didn't drop her in the throne room, but back in the privacy of the room she'd shared with Syrus. Forest was grateful for her father's discretion. She went into the bathroom and splashed some cold water on her face. Her hands began to ache as the hilt of her sword beckoned them. She took one deep breath and looked herself in the eyes. Her life was changing rapidly. A smile pulled into the side of her mouth. It was time for Leith's reckoning.

Forest started down the stairs, the key gripped tightly in her hand. She passed a few different people in the halls, all of them gasped and gave her little bows. She moved on without acknowledging them. Her eyes landed on Merhl standing next to the door of her target.

He stepped forward and sank down onto his knees grabbing her hands. "I'm so sorry, Milady. I failed."

"What are you talking about?"

"He's gone. His father came, threatened to kill a hostage. He knocked me unconscious."

Forest looked alarmingly at the door. "No." she shook her head. "No!" Charging past him, she thrust the key into the lock that wasn't locked at all and pushed the door open.

Empty.

She closed her eyes and hung her head. Damn it. Well, he'd gotten loose from her before, slippery bastard. She sighed and left the room.

"Please forgive me, Milady. I should have rather died than opened the door, but I feared for the life Vladien threatened. And now my life is forfeit anyway."

"It is not!" Forest said forcefully.

"But surely once Rahaxeris learns of my inefficiency, he'll…"

"He won't harm you, Merhl. I'll talk to him. You needn't fear for your life."

Redge came around the corner. "Forest, you're back. I see you've learned of our little mishap."

She gave Merhl a reassuring squeeze on the arm before turning to Redge. "I want this investigated quietly. Take down Vladien if you find him, and arrest any of his accomplices. But do not pursue Leith."

Redge raised one eyebrow. "Might I ask why?"

"There's no need. He's a coward. He needs to feel safe. He'll come to me. He always does."

"And if we apprehend Vladien and Leith is with him? What then?"

"Arrest him and bring him to my office."

Redge took a closer stock of her, noticing the stone around her neck, feeling its subtle effects around her. "Your office?"

Forest smiled. "In Fortress castle. As of today, everyone in Fortress will know the location of the office of Hailemarris. I'll be easy to find."

Redge returned her smile. "Hailemarris, eh? Congratulations. Does Syrus know?"

"Of course."

He gave her a little bow. "I'll keep you informed of our progress in the investigation, Milady."

"Thanks."

Chapter Twenty-three

Forest walked through the front entrance of Fortress, as she had countless times in the past, yet now, it was different, dreamlike. She didn't have to pass through security check points and have her name and race blazed across her chest for all to see. She strode into the main lobby, her head erect, eager to prove herself. She let her anxiety and anger about Leith fade into the background of her mind, comforted in the knowledge that when he showed his face again she'd cut it clean off without hesitation.

The people milling around and waiting in line to speak to the receptionist parted like the red sea as Baal strode through the room toward Forest.

"Nice to see you again, Baal," she said easily.

"And you as well. There's a lot stewing around here. I think it best I show you to your office before I say more."

"Lead on."

Forest assumed the stewing he referred to centered around her showing up in her new professional capacity. She smiled to herself, unconcerned by the postulating and posturing she was sure the high council was doing at that very moment.

Baal led her down a hallway lined with the doors to the offices of the highest ranking. A little thrill shivered up her spine at the thought that she would be counted among them.

The highly polished door loomed before her at the very end of the hall. A carved sign hung at eyelevel. It read: The Office of Hailemarris. Supreme Judge of the New Republic of Regia. By appointment only.

Baal opened the door for her. It was a beautiful room, furnished exquisitely, but she felt a little let down, thinking it would be bigger.

Baal laughed, drawing her attention. "Disappointed?"

"Oh, no." Forest checked herself. "It's lovely."

Baal laughed again. "This is just the front room, for your secretary. Your actual office space is behind that door."

The door blended seamlessly with the wall, but his finger directed her to see the doorknob. She opened the door, and that dreamlike quality flowed over her again. Everything was in shades of green. The desk reminded her of the locker that used to be downstairs, beautifully carved; the four legs each looked like trees, the surface supported by the branches. The space eased and brought clarity to her thoughts. She sat down at her desk, overwhelmed. "So, who is my secretary?"

"That's for you to decide. Actually, you will probably want a secretary *and* a personal assistant. I might recommend that you choose the assistant with some careful consideration, someone you trust."

Forest smiled. "I know who I want...You were going to tell me about some trouble before?"

"Yes. The members of the high council are assembled and squabbling about you right now."

"Well, seeing as I'm their new boss, I guess I better get in there and break it up."

Baal cocked his brow and smirked. "May I come along?"

"Sure. You're my wingman."

"Your what?"

Forest stood up and strode past him. "Never mind."

She marched directly into the room and the middle of a garble of arguing voices. All eyes turned to her, and the fighting died comically. She looked at each of them in turn before taking a seat in the circle. "Well, sit down. I don't have all day."

Kindel, standing in the back of the room, had to cover his laugh with a coughing fit.

Baal walked to stand beside Kindel, drawing nervous glances as the council took their seats.

Everyone seemed highly agitated except Nahcaan, whose chair groaned under his five hundred pounds as he leaned back nonchalantly.

Before anyone could say anything, Forest launched in. "You all know who I am, even if you've never spoke to me before. And you all know what I am now. Change can be jarring and upsetting. I don't care what you think of me, or how you think the world should be run. I didn't start the war that was the catalyst to all of this. All of us must adapt, and we must now answer for our actions of the past."

Both Lush and Zefyre shifted uncomfortably and glanced at each other.

"Over the next few days, I will be meeting one on one with each of you…It is time for us all to set aside our own agendas. Fortress will support and enforce the laws of the New Republic. You will evolve, or else find your job terminated. Are we clear?"

"Yes, Madam Hailemarris," Zefyre said.

The others followed suit and parroted her.

"You are dismissed."

No one moved.

Forest cleared her throat. "As of now, the council shall not meet in here unless it is a meeting I have called. If you chose to socialize with each other outside of work, that is your business. Now go back to your offices and get to work."

"Yes, Madam," they grumbled.

Forest sat still as they all began to file out.

"Hold on, Kindel."

Kindel sat down next to her and waited quietly until the room was empty except for Baal. He let his laughter come out, and he slapped her on the shoulder. "Where did that come from?"

Forest laughed too. "I don't know. It just fell out of my mouth. I guess I've wanted to tell them all off for a long time."

"You did awesome."

"Thanks. How would you like to come work for me? As my personal assistant?"

Kindel leaned back in his chair smiling. "I'd expect a raise from my current pay grade and four weeks paid vacation every year."

"Three."

"Done."

They chuckled and shook hands on it. "Thanks, Kindel. I appreciate it."

"I'm honored, Forest."

"I bet you never thought I'd be your boss."

He looked at her seriously. "I wouldn't wager too much on that bet."

Forest squeezed his hand. "Get your stuff and move it to my office. I expect you know where it is."

"Ha! That I do. We've all been suffering with the racket of construction for weeks."

Forest pinched herself on the way back to her office. She sank back down behind her beautiful desk and sighed. The adrenaline rush from speaking to the high council members burned off, leaving her light-headed. Baal continued to hang around like a bodyguard.

After a little while, Kindel came in carrying boxes.

"I've got something I need you to do, Kindel."

He set the boxes in a corner. "All right."

"Well, it seems I need a secretary for the front office. And I'm not paying your rate for you to do that work."

"Have someone in mind?"

"Yeah. Ena. She's a servant in the Onyx Castle. Would you go and present her with my job offer?"

"No problem. I'll go there now."

****

Kindel found himself feeling more optimistic than he had in longer than he could remember as he walked through the halls of the Onyx Castle. Nothing really looked different, but the inhabitants moved about more cautiously. And where his visits to the Vampire's castle had been infrequent before and those who lived there treated him as inferior, now, despite that he was obviously not a member of the *Rune-dy*, the fact that he was an elf, afforded him a new measure of respect.

He was about to grab the next female he saw and ask her where he could find Ena when he spotted Redge walking toward him, his nose stuck in a file. Kindel didn't know Redge very well, but what he did know earned his respect.

"Redge."

Redge looked up at Kindel, the frown on his face easing into a smile. "Kindel." He nodded. "What brings you here? The council send you?"

"No, not the council, Forest. Or Madam Hailemarris I should say."

"Ah yes. She told me about that. How is she managing so far?"

Kindel told Redge the short version of what had happened that morning in Fortress.

"Well, here," Redge said handing the files he'd been looking at to Kindel. "These are actually for Forest. They contain my initial findings of the investigation she asked me to conduct. I didn't even know where to find her, but since you work for her now…Tell her I'll come around and see her in a few days to report."

Kindel tucked the files under his arm. "Okay…So, now what does the future hold for you?"

Redge sighed. "I wish I knew. I have no idea what I'll be doing or in what capacity. Syrus doesn't need me anymore. I'm not sure the military is a right fit for me anymore either."

"You might consider joining us over at Fortress."

Redge shrugged. "Maybe."

Kindel extended his hand. "I'll see you in a few days then, when you call on Forest. Oh, and could you tell me where I can find a young woman named Ena?"

Redge sent him in the right direction to Ena, who enthusiastically accepted the job offer as soon as he mentioned Forest's name. She followed him so closely, he almost tripped three different times. Anxious to get back to Fortress, Kindle was stopped dead in his tracks by a young ogre.

"Please, sir, you work for the Lady Forest, do you not?"

"How do you know that?"

The ogre looked flustered. "Ogre's know everything that is said in the Onyx Castle."

Kindle smirked. "And you are?"

"Merhl, sir. I owe the Lady Forest a great debt. Please see that she gets this."

Merhl thrust a small sealed envelope into Kindel's free hand.

Kindel came back to Forest's office with an excited Ena practically bouncing in his wake. Forest didn't really know how to train her, seeing as she'd never done that type of work herself, so she let Kindel get her settled.

He stuck his head back in her office a little while later. "I almost forgot, while I was at the Onyx Castle, Merhl the ogre, gave me this to give to you. And here is a preliminary report on the investigation you had Redge do."

He placed a sealed envelope and the files on the desk and left the room. Forest opened the envelope first. Inside was a short letter and a shimmery End of the Bridge. His handwriting was barely legible.

The note read: *To the Lady Forest, I'm so sorry for failing you. I know I can never atone for it. I hope you accept this gift along with my continued apology. It is not a normal End of the Bridge. I made it special for you. You can use it over and over and it will take you to wherever you desire to go at the time. All you have to do is think of where you want to go as you hold it. I hope you find it useful. And again, I'm sorry. –Merhl*

Forest picked up the little thing and looked at it for a second before pocketing it. "That's handy," she said to herself.

She turned her attention to the file sent from Redge and was astounded at his speed and efficiency. Of course, he hadn't unearthed everything in the few short hours since she'd seen him, but what he had discovered made her head spin. She'd need time to consider what to do about the knowledge there.

"Kindel," she called through the wall.

He stuck his head around the door. "Yes."

"I need to issue arrest warrants. Can you do that? I don't know how."

"Sure. Who are we going after?"

"Vladien and...Dracula."

Kindel flashed a broad, amused smile. "Dracula, huh?"

Forest groaned and put her head in her hands. "It's only my first day."

"I knew you'd waste no time stickin' it to 'em."

Kindel left the office, and Forest went back to contemplating how to structure the new judiciary system. She made notes, borrowing from her knowledge of past Regian practices and what she knew of American policies. The *Rune-dy's* library came to her mind, and she wondered what she might learn of the justice systems of other worlds. Determined nothing she created would be corrupt, broken, or inefficient, Forest didn't realize how long she'd been working when Kindel popped his head in again.

"We didn't discuss my hours, but I was hoping I could go home before the moon hits its zenith."

Forest glanced around the room, noticing for the first time there was no window. "I'm sorry. Is Ena still working?"

"Yeah. We've been waiting for you. I wouldn't worry about her, though. She's still giddy with excitement." Kindel came over and laid a hand on her shoulder. "Go home and get some rest. It's just your first day. The job will be here tomorrow, and the day after, and the day after that."

Forest nodded and put her notes in the desk drawer. "I'll go home soon. Please make sure Ena gets back to the Onyx Castle safely."

"No problem."

Forest locked her office an hour later and walked out into the deserted lobby, Baal walking beside her.

"You did good today," he said. "I'll be here at your disposal for the next few days."

"Thanks, Baal. I appreciate it."

He waited while she told the ogre by the entrance where she wanted to go. Forest waved to him as she stepped into the blackness.

The weight of the day crashed onto her shoulders as the portal dropped her in the fringe close to her house. She wished Syrus was there. Her stress lifted a fraction as she entered her garden.

"Hello? I'm back. Netriet?" she called as she unlocked the front door.

The house was dark and empty. Forest switched on the lights and went through the house. Netriet was gone. Forest was disappointed. She'd wanted to tell Netriet about what she'd done and how things went since she'd left.

She went back outside. "Netriet?"

Nothing.

Forest shrugged and went back inside, locking the door behind her. Was she gone for good, or would she come back?

Exhaustion took over. She turned the lights out on her way to the bedroom, pulled off her boots and sword, and fell onto the bed, fully clothed. "Syrus," she sighed before falling deeply asleep.

****

Rahaxeris crossed his arms and surveyed Syrus across the table.

"So?" Syrus asked.

"I think it's a great idea, Syrus. I've got all kinds of information about such things." He stood and walked over to the wall of books, scanning the titles. "Here we go. This one."

Rahaxeris set the heavy tome on the table in front of Syrus. Syrus clenched his eyes shut and muttered his new incantation a few times before looking down at the words and pictures. Rahaxeris let him read for a few moments in silence.

"Here. This is the right thing," Syrus said turning the book toward Rahaxeris. "Can you make those?"

Rahaxeris looked. "No problem. Just give me a few minutes."

Syrus waited as Rahaxeris went into another room. He came back with a small sealed box. "Here you go. Both are in there."

Syrus tucked the box into his cloak. "Thank you."

"Don't mention it…By the way, your sight intrigues me. You're able to see by your own words."

"Yeah. It doesn't last, and it's not very clear. But I've been changing up the words, and sometimes I get more time or more color."

"Maxcarion offered no help when you sought him?"

"That's right. He said my blindness was permanent."

"Hmm. Sounds like you hold the key to your sight within you. Maybe you just haven't figured out the right combination to heal your eyes completely. You should keep trying."

Syrus contemplated. "Perhaps you're right. I will keep trying."

Rahaxeris opened a portal for him back to the Obsidian Mountain. He landed at the base and began the long climb up to his room, his prize tucked safely next to his chest. Ithiel, Guyas, and Taurus were in their nightfall mediations and didn't come out to greet him. He rested his elbows on the window ledge in his room, his sight sliding back into darkness. He didn't want to sleep on the floor, alone. He wanted to sleep wrapped around Forest. The constant pain of separation pricked and stung.

She'd had her first day of work and yet they weren't together, celebrating. She said she would kill Leith as soon as she accepted her title, and she'd accepted it. Rahaxeris had confirmed it. Her slave mark would be gone. His mind flooded with images of making love to her for the first time as a free woman. The fantasy overwhelmed his body. His feet weren't nailed to the floor. What the hell was he doing here?

He turned around and headed back out the door he just entered. Halfway down the stairs he stopped. His hair stood on end, goose bumps spreading over his skin. Icy fear dropped into his stomach as intuition piqued. Syrus continued down the stairs in a break-neck run.

Chapter Twenty-four

Forest nestled down into her pillow, dreaming. *She looked up, surrounded by trees, as dark clouds spread over the sky. The wind howled and beat down on the trees, their branches cracking from the strain. Scraping and crumbling noise filled her ears and as the trees continued to break, they began to scream. Forest covered her ears as the screaming grew louder, and louder, and louder…*

Forest woke up, the sound of her alarm screeching. She sighed, annoyed, and clambered off the bed. How had Netriet tripped it again? Forest rubbed her eyes as she opened the front door and stepped out into the velvet darkness. Full lucidity had not yet taken a hold of her. She squinted at the gate. No one was there. Her eyes darted over to the flashing red lights on her alarm system. Forest ran and punched in the code, silencing it.

She turned a full circle, now fully alert. Her heart galloping up to her throat, blocking her breathing, as her eyes landed on it. There, on her stone wall, drawn in blood, was the design that used to disfigure her neck and shoulder: her slave mark entwined with the seven crescent lovers marks.

The front door of her house stood open, creaking on its hinge. Her eyes darted around again. Her tree that stood close to the wall had two broken limbs. Leith must have scaled the wall. His laugh sounded from inside the house before he stepped into the light of the doorway, smiling, and holding her sword.

Unarmed, she had no choice. Forest ran. She ducked under the archway and out into the woods before he'd taken two steps in pursuit. She heard him follow. She circled around the backside of her property. Stopping behind a tree trunk, listening. He was quieter than she knew he could be. The hammering of her pulse made it harder for her to hear minute noises.

She'd never feared him like this before. He wasn't here to rape her. He was going to kill her. Her scar began to burn. Forest bit down on her knuckle to keep from crying out in pain. What was he doing to cause her this pain? Lava ran through her veins.

The sound of his quiet footfalls sounded to her right. Forest pushed off from her hiding place and bolted, the heat rising up her neck, spreading into her skull. Her vision doubled.

"How does that feel, love?" his taunt sounded behind her. "You should have killed me when you had the chance."

The heat was unbearable. If she would have had a weapon, she'd have cut open her head to relieve the volcanic pressure. Her steps faltered as black spots popped up in her blurry double vision. He was behind her.

She faced Leith, pulling her hair. "What are you doing to me?"

"You're my slave. I'm ordering you to feel what I want you to feel. You see how benevolent I've been to you all these years, how loving. I could have inflicted this kind of pain on you any time I wished, but I never wanted to hurt you, love."

Forest turned to run again…but she couldn't move. An odd feeling pinned her to the spot. She looked down. Her sword, bright with blood, protruded from her stomach. It didn't hurt so much, she thought, until he twisted the blade to the side.

Forest's scream rang through the trees.

Leith put a hand on her back and pushed. Forest slid down the length of the blade to the ground. He threw the sword aside and turned her over, face up. He straddled her and sat down on her wound.

She couldn't breathe. The world dimmed. *I'm dying.*

Leith leaned close and kissed her bloody mouth. "I'm breaking up with you, Forest. I'm sorry it couldn't work. We're just too different. It's not you, it's me."

Her time was closing in. He kissed her again, a tear falling from one of his eyes. "I did love you, Forest. I gotta hand it to you. You almost beat me. You would have, if it weren't for your love for me. Your love stopped you again and again."

Forest's vision jittered for a second, and then everything went smooth, too smooth. Colors began to bleed into one another. She closed her eyes. She didn't want Leith's face to be the last thing she saw. Syrus reached out to her in the ebony abyss, and she floated to him.

Chapter Twenty-Five

Leith gazed down at Forest, her lifeblood running from her body into the thirsty ground. He wasn't happy about it. He hated having to break his doll.

A roar of rage and agony blasted through the woods like a shockwave. Leith jumped and turned around, instantly caught in the grip of hands so strong, his bones broke under the fingers.

Leith's cry for mercy landed on deaf ears. He jerked and squirmed as electric objects entered his body from the hands that held him. His icy eyes met the hard steel of Syrus'. He recognized his captor.

"So, you're the one who took her from me, cousin…You're too late, Syrus. She's dead."

Syrus didn't bother releasing Leith to pull his short swords from his belt. He opened his palms and filled Leith's body with sphere after sphere of his rage. And the second he was full, Syrus broke them all open, shattering through Leith's body like glass.

Leith fell to the ground, eight-ball hemorrhages in his eyes, long jagged cracks snaking over every inch of his skin, bleeding out.

Syrus lifted Forest off the ground and carried her back to her garden. The magic at the gate let them through. He fell to his knees, clutching her to him, and wept. "Forest, don't leave me," he whispered. "Please. Please. I cannot live without you."

He laid her gently on the ground and placed his hand over her wound. The same words he used to regain his sight, he now chanted over her, pulsing power from his palm into her injury. He'd never tried using his power to heal.

Her heart beat languorously. Syrus felt every slowed beat through his body. Then it stalled and stopped.

"NO!"

Syrus gathered her against him again, red lightening cracking over his whole body. The electric current engulfed Forest, the lightening streaming into her wound like water to a drain. Moving up through her veins, jolting her silent heart.

Forest's eyes shot open. A scream exploding from her lungs.

Relief such as he had never known flooded Syrus. His tears fell on her face as she looked up at him.

She reached up and placed her hand on his cheek. "Syrus..." She winced, a weak gasp of pain sliding from her lips as her slave mark broke open, bled, and then sealed back together, her flesh new and perfect.

Her stomach wound began pulling itself together under Syrus' hand. Her eyelids fluttered, her eyes sliding backward, and her hand fell from his face as she dropped into unconsciousness.

Chapter Twenty-Six

Forest opened her eyes in the darkness to the familiar sounds and scents of her bedroom. Had it all been a dream? A terrible, terrible dream? She moved her hand to trace along her scar… but there was no scar. She exhaled, feeling the bruised weakness in her core. She turned her head. She was in her bed, Syrus silhouetted in the dark, asleep next to her.

Syrus had known she was in danger. He'd saved her life.

Forest sat up, her hands involuntarily clutched at her stomach. The vision of her sword coming from her flesh flashed before her eyes. She shivered. The image was a terror that would stick with her the rest of her life.

But Leith was dead. The knowledge brought a strange twinge. She placed her feet silently on the floor and crept out of the house. Compelled to see his body, to have her eyes confirm what her new skin already had, Forest walked through her garden and out. The moon cast its light on the woods around her. She'd lost time, unaware of how long she'd been out. His body may have fallen to ash by now, or Syrus may have done something with it.

It was closure she craved. Just a private minute to say goodbye.

Leith's mangled body lay face up. The aquamarine moonlight reflected on the surface of his eyes. The areas of his skin that were undamaged held the appearance of wet wax. She starred at him, momentarily numb.

The numbness didn't last. Forest choked on the vomit rising up her throat as all of her memories of him from the first to the last flashed through her mind. She fell to her knees next to his body, shaking with silent tears and held his hand, his fingernails crumbling to dust at her touch.

"It didn't have to be like this," she whispered. "I'd have given you my love freely, if only you'd have asked for it. If only you could have been kind...if only..."

The memories of how her marks confused her heart stung in her chest. However forced, false, and twisted it had been, she had loved him. And it could have been real, if only he would have been content with the free gift of love. But he wanted property rights.

Forest moved through every emotion she'd ever had regarding Leith, setting each one free like a bird to the wind. Decades of weight lifted from her little by little as she opened her hands and released the past. But another sinking feeling swooped into her stomach. She turned her head around abruptly. Syrus was standing behind her. A pain worse than being stabbed, worse than death, sank into her heart, transferred from Syrus.

****

His eyes didn't deceive him. He'd never seen clearer without human blood. But how Syrus wished what he saw was a cruel illusion. She shed tears for Leith. *Tears!* With plain regret in her heart. And the words she'd uttered, he'd have traded anything to un-hear them.

Betrayal. Betrayal too deep to pardon. Everything within him that lived for her...died. His heart shut down in self-preservation, and he went cold inside. He took a step back and lifted his hands in surrender. "Well, I guess I wasn't supposed to see this. By all means, continue telling his corpse how you love him and you wish you were bound to him and not me."

"What? Syrus, that's not—"

"Not what? True? You've pushed me away and pushed me away, rejecting my heart over and over. You've held me at arm's length, and you let him live when you had the chance to end it. How can you say you love me when you obviously love him, and how can you love him in the first place?"

"Syrus, please—"

"No, don't worry about it, this one's on me. I'm the fool who thought underneath it all, you actually loved me."

"I do!"

"That's a damn shame. If it's true...this is going to hurt, a lot."

"What's going to..." Forest's voice trailed off as Syrus closed her access off to his heart.

Forest gaped at him, unable to breath. He was rejecting her as his mate. The legendary pain of such a thing rushed on Forest. The invisible ties between them pulled and tore like hacking off a limb but leaving it hanging by a sinew, still connected, but dead. Her eyes, hands, and heart ripped apart under the surface as he turned his back and walked away.

Forest didn't move. It hadn't really happened she told herself. Amazingly, the pain of rejection, at least the physical part of it, was already fading. How could that be when all the stories told of enduring agony? That individuals who rejected their life mates suffered lifelong excruciation? It wasn't some searing sting or burning leaving her writhing on the ground; it quickly settled into despair and desolation sliding through her veins, poisoning every inch of her.

I can live with it. It's not that bad.

She continued to watch his retreating back. He walked at a steady pace, his frame completely ridged, until she could no longer see him at all.

Strange. This is what I wanted, right? Isn't it? To be free of anyone and everything. To live my life without the burden of hurting him because I can't be what he wants. To let him go. Never see him again. Never touch him. Never hear his voice teasing me. Never again see his childlike smile. What I want...I? What I want?

When did I become so damn noble?

Forest rubbed her hands together. The pull of their bond still existed in her palms, like a ghost, a mere phantom of what had been there. But it was still there!

Get off your ass, stupid!

Forest jumped to her feet, grabbed her sword from the ground next to Leith's body, and ran for her life.

The moonlight slid along the blade as it shot through the air, missing Syrus' head by an inch, sticking deep into the trunk of a tree next to him. He whirled around as she came up behind him, his eyes bugging with shock.

"Where do you think you're going, sucker?" she demanded.

"Forest…what are…what do you…" he spluttered.

"You're not going to just walk out of my life. Especially when your reasons are ass backwards."

"What?"

"You misunderstood what you saw, what you heard. I came outside to see his body with my own eyes. After all the years of being tied to him, everything he's done to me, I needed closure."

"You were grieving! I felt it!"

"Yeah I was grieving, but not his death, you idiot! I was grieving for my own life, and what he did to it. I was letting the past go so we could move ahead. Sometimes a woman just needs to cry."

"Bullshit, I know what I heard. I can't take anymore. It's over." He ducked under her blade and continued walking away.

Forest pulled her sword from the tree trunk and ran to block his path. She thrust the blade under his chin.

"Get out of my way, Forest." He took a step back from the blade.

She advanced, keeping the sword's edge a breath from his jugular. "No. We'll have it out here and now, and this is the only way I know how."

"I'm not going to fight you."

"Damn it, Syrus! Draw your weapons!"

When he made no move, she threw her sword on the ground and grabbed one of his, pulling it from its sheath and pushing it into his hand. He sighed, gripping it loosely. She picked her sword back up and instantly launched into a ferocious attack. Syrus stumbled back, forced to block her strikes.

He evaded, his eyes bugging worse than before. "Are you trying to kill me?"

"You've been in my memories, Syrus. You know how his lover marks altered my emotional responses. I never wanted to hurt you or drive a wedge between us. I felt unworthy of you, and I made myself believe that you were ashamed of me. I wanted more time to make something of myself. I want to be considered your equal. That's why I accepted my birthright."

Syrus gaped at her. "*That's* why you accepted your birthright?" His shock had him lowering his guard.

Forest wasn't having it. She gritted her teeth and attacked harder. "I lied," she shouted over the clanging of metal. "I'm an ungrateful liar. I've lied to my heart, but my heart never believed me. No matter how many times I repeated the lie, my heart dismissed it as blasphemy. "

Syrus moved forward, drawing his second sword, letting his feelings pour out into his blades. Forest ducked a vicious strike and spun away, regaining her footing, pushing back on him.

"I tuned out the truth just as I tuned out your heart. I ran from you because I wanted you so much. I wanted to be yours from the first moment I laid eyes on you, Syrus! But I couldn't forget my lifelong conditioning that I was nothing but trash."

Her sword clashed so hard against his, the bones of his arm rattled. "Stop fighting me!" he shouted.

"You can run away, but I'll catch you. You can let go of me, but I won't let go of you!"

A strangled cry sounded from her lungs and she struck at him as hard as she could, her every word punctuated with a clang of metal. "I. Won't. Let. You. Go!"

Syrus' heart shocked back to life. *There she is, my Forest.*

The hurt and anger on Syrus' face drained, and he let his arms hang at his sides.

"NO!" She shouted, dropping her sword and grabbing one of his hands bringing the tip of his blade to her heart. "Don't stop!"

He tried to pull away, appalled, but she held his hand fast.

"If you leave, you may as well kill me right now. I won't survive you, Syrus."

"Forest..." he rasped, pulling his hand from hers, dropping his swords and grabbing her by the shoulders.

Tears ran down her cheeks. "I thought you'd always be there," she sobbed. "I thought I could put you aside and pick you up when I was ready and you'd be okay with that. I abused you so you'd go away, thinking it was best for both of us, all the while not really believing you'd ever reject me. But you have. All I can feel is the absence of our bond. I thought I didn't want it and that I was just too afraid of the pain to really reject you."

"Are you in pain?" he asked.

"Yes, it's just not what I thought. It's not the pain that's driving me to say this. I want it back, Syrus. I want you! You set me free. I'm a free woman. I want to start over."

Syrus shook his head sadly. Desperately she grabbed his hand and laid it over her heart. "Do you doubt me?"

His brow creased in a frown. Her heart hammered against her ribs. "Can you still feel it at all? Even a trace?"

"Yes," he whispered. "Oh, Forest what have I done? I'm looking right in your eyes, it's blurry, but I can see you and our bond's not healing."

Hope leapt into her throat. "Do you want it to?"

He hung his head, his shoulders slumping. "Yes. I want it, but I destroyed it."

She held both his hands tightly in hers. "I don't care. As long as we're together, bond or no, I love you."

"I don't know…"

He pulled away from her and closed his eyes. She could feel him slipping away from her yet again. She had to do something…Forest reached into her pocket, her fingers closing around the End of the Bridge Merhl gave her. She moved to Syrus and reached out for him.

"Will you come with me, Syrus?"

"Huh?"

Forest wrapped her arms tightly around his waist, the End of the Bridge, clasped in her fist and thought of where she wanted to go. The portal opened around them sucking them into the darkness. The end dropped them in midair ten feet above the water.

The silvery purple light of the water closed over them as they fell through the surface. Forest stroked to the top, gasping for air. Syrus coughed and shook the water from his hair.

"You could have given me a little more warning what you were up to, Forest. Geez."

She swam to him and framed his face between her palms. "Look where we are."

"I've noticed."

She turned her head toward the crescent rock, where the small waterfalls fell into the river. "Come with me."

They swam to the falls, to the rock ledge, waist deep, the shimmering water spraying up around them. Forest faced Syrus, who watched her warily. "I want to start over. Let's go back to when we stood right here. Remember?"

"Yes," he whispered. "I remember."

Forest gripped his shoulders. "Oh, Syrus. I'm sorry. I went about everything wrong. Please…is there nothing left in your heart for me?"

He hung his head, rubbing the heel of his hand over his chest. "It hurts so much. It's still yours, it always will be no matter what I do…I want to trust you, but…"

"Please," she whispered laying her hand over his heart, "give me the chance to heal it."

He took a deep breath and rested his forehead against hers. It would take time, she realized. He held himself aloof from her, but he was here.

"I'm sorry I misunderstood," he said.

"I'm sorry I ever left your side for a second."

"I'd give anything to change it."

"So would I."

They clung to each other, tears racking their bodies.

"Kiss me, Syrus."

He took a deep breath and framed her face gently with his hands. His gaze pushed deep as he rested his forehead against hers. His bottom lip trembled. "Are you finally done running from me?"

"Yes, Syrus. Yes!"

He leaned in, his lips a breath from hers and stopped. Her eyes fluttered, and she titled her head back, her lips begging his. He eased in but still made no contact. "Are you sure?" he whispered.

"Yes."

Syrus ran his thumb over her aching bottom lip. "Are you really sure?"

Her blood began screaming for him, burning through her veins. "I swear."

His lips came down so slowly and so soft. Forest's eyes shut tight, and her face pulled in the tension of pleasure. He patiently built such terrible agony inside her. Flames and starving hunger.

They both gasped; a quickening in their hearts shimmered silver. Hope sprang a well in Forest, the connection was healing. The pain around his eyes eased, and he breathed easier.

He kissed her again, harder. "The bond is alive. It's battered and fragile, but it lives."

"I felt it, too."

A faint trace of his innocent smile broke his lips. He crushed her against him and pulled her under the falls into the cave. They dove at each other. Forest's shirt ripped under his urgency to touch her new skin. His fingers ran down her neck, over her shoulder, and down to her elbow where her scar used to be. He replaced his fingers with his lips. "You're mine?"

"Yes, I'm yours, Syrus. Completely."

Steam filled the cave, rising off their bare skin as they truly made love for the first time. Every physical act they had shared before paled in comparison. Every wish and yearning fulfilled without haste, overawed with love. Every second the bond gained strength, resurrecting in their hands, breathing deeply in their hearts. Only the eyes held back, something still hindering the connection there.

After exhaustion claimed them both, Forest rested her head on his shoulder and watched the dancing light on the cave walls as it bounced off the water.

"There are no words, Syrus," she said still breathless.

He shook his head in agreement. "No. None that could adequately describe..."

"You can mark me now."

"I thought you wanted some time to be free of scars."

She did. She never wanted another scar unless she won it in battle. But her remorse urged her on, trying to continue to make amends. "It's okay... I'm ready."

Syrus brought her hand to his lips. "That means the world to me. But I'll have to decline."

"What?"

"Thanks, but no thanks. I've got an alternative for you." He looked around for his discarded cloak. Squinting, his vision fading, he spotted it floating in the corner of the cave. He grabbed it and retrieved the small box still tucked safely in the inside pocket.

He handed it to her. She opened the lid. Two gold rings lay inside.

"Oh, Syrus."

"Learning a little about Earthly customs presented the perfect solution. Now you can mark me too, and you can take it off anytime you like."

She grabbed his left hand and slid the larger ring onto his finger. He followed her example. Her heart swelled again, and she wrapped her arms around his neck. "It's perfect, Syrus. I love you, today and forever."

"And I love you. Today and forever, Forest... Please don't stay away from me again."

"Oh, I think you'll find me around a little too much for your liking."

He gave her a mock grimace. "You mean I'll have to see you every day?"

"Yup."

"How tedious." His expression grew serious. "I'm going to regain my sight Forest, permanently. I'm close to unlocking it."

"That's wonderful."

He caressed her face. "I want to look at you all the time. Your beauty, your true face, is one of the greatest gifts of my whole life, second only to your heart."

She placed her palm flat on his chest, his heart beating against it. She marveled at the blessing he was and how she had almost lost him. "Your love saved me, in every way. I won't fear happiness ever again." She sealed her words with a kiss. "I'm getting cold. Let's go home."

Syrus sighed contentedly. "Ah, home. Yes."

They collected their wet clothes and ducked out from under the falls.

"We should come back here regularly," he said.

"Definitely."

The End of the Bridge took them back to Forest's garden. She looked nervously at Syrus. "You did know this is where I meant when I said 'home' right?"

He smiled easily. "Of course. Where else?"

They entered the house together. Forest turned and looked at him. He held an armful of wet garments that dripped water on the floor. Oblivious to the mess he was making, just like a guy. She sighed and shook her head.

"What?" he said defensively.

"You're gonna clean that up."

He smirked and dropped the pile on the floor. "Yeah, I'm right on top of that."

"Sucker." The word may have been insulting, but her tone was clearly adoring.

He jumped and caught her against him before she could think to run away. She giggled and he kissed her. They were home. Nothing had ever felt more right.

The rest of the night was filled with gentleness, gentle touches and gentle words. Forest fell off to sleep just before the sunrise.

Syrus lay next to her, running his fingertips along the planes of her back as she slept. Dawn broke through the curtains, casting a shimmering light on Forest's skin, but Syrus could barely see it. He gritted his teeth, a swift anger flaring inside him. He'd been deprived long enough, and he had an idea about what was still wrong with their bond.

He got silently out of bed. He found his damp pants and slipped them on before heading out into the dawn.

The sound of the door closing roused Forest. She rolled over into the empty space next to her. "Syrus?" She sat up, forcing her eyes open.

The house was silent.

Groaning, she climbed out of bed and went to the closet to get her robe. She padded out into the living room, suddenly alarmed.

She felt something…odd. It took a moment before she realized she was feeling something transferred from Syrus.

Forest looked out the window and saw him. He was sitting in the middle of the garden in a meditative pose, all of his muscles taut, and his face pulled into a mask of pain. His heartbeat sounded inside her head, strong and steady.

Forest choked on her own breath as his pulse palpitated for a second then sped up. His racing heart thundered in her ears. Her internal alarm went off as his vital signs faltered.

"SYRUS!" She ran from the house, skidding and falling to her knees in front of him. She grabbed his shoulders and shook him. "Syrus! Stop!"

Red lightening cracked and snaked over his whole body, shocking her hands. She pulled them back, burned. His mouth moved, uttering unintelligible words over and over.

"Syrus, *please! Please stop!*"

His body went rigid and pulled tight like a cable. The strain under the surface looked as though it was about to break him to pieces. Forest grabbed him again, ignoring the burn, and shook him as hard as she could. His head fell back as his eyelids opened. Lightning struck inside his eyes. His body lifted off the ground, suspended.

A terrible shattering filled the air and Syrus fell back to the ground, unconscious.

Forest threw herself on him weeping. "What have you done?" she cried. "Come back to me." She laid her head on his chest, her tears pooling on his sternum. His heartbeat, irregular and feeble.

"Syrus, wake up. Please, please wake up." She clung to him.

Time passed, clouds covered the morning sky. Rain pelted them, rising steam off Syrus' burning hot skin. Forest slipped into a semi-comatose state, unable to handle what happened.

Her awareness broke through as his hand ran over the back of her head.

Forest gasped and lifted her head. He sat up a little and looked straight at her. Knives of fire shot into the center of Forest's eyes. The connection roared to life in blinding red light, lighting their hands and hearts and souls in a new connection, stronger than the first. Unbreakable, imperishable, and immortal.

"Oh, Syrus what have you done?"

His pupils were open, the pearl gray of his eyes shimmered, and a thin red line circled the inner rim of his iris.

"I've done it, Forest! I've healed my eyes." He got to his knees holding her face in his hands. "I can see you, Forest...I can see you perfectly. Shh..." he whispered, wiping her tears off her cheeks.

"Why did you do it? You put your life in danger. How could you be so stupid? It's not worth that."

He titled her head back a little so she couldn't evade his gaze. The spiritual connection binding their eyes flared and shimmered. His stare, so intense, reached down into her soul, as it never had before.

"Don't say it wasn't worth the risk. Look at me."

"I am."

"No, look deeper. You feel that?"

"Yes."

"Do you see it? Do you see my soul?"

Forest trembled and shook her head. "I...I don't know..."

"You're holding back. Don't be afraid."

I am afraid.

Forest took a breath and let go, instantly astonished. There was nowhere for her to hide now. All that she was broke open to him, and all that he was broke open to her. Their sprits embraced.

"Oh, yes, Syrus. I see…It's beautiful…I never knew intimacy could be this deep. It's amazing."

He ran his thumb over her bottom lip. "This face has haunted me for so long, driving me to madness while I was in the dark. There never was a more beautiful creature, Forest."

She folded into his arms. "That's exactly the way I feel about you."

"And now I finally have you."

She nestled closer. "Forever."

Chapter Twenty-Seven

One month later

Forest stared at herself in the mirror and decided to change her outfit again, for the sixth time. Syrus came up behind her, wrapped his arms around her waist, and pressed his lips into her neck. Her nerves calmed as she leaned back against him.

"I'm telling you, you should go with the blue. It looks official but not cold."

"All right," Forest conceded. "What are you wearing?"

"My same old, same old. No one expects a mage to be dressed in anything other than monk-ish stuff."

"Lucky you."

"You better hurry up, Madam Hailemarris, or you'll be late."

The idea of being late kicked her heart rate up. She took a deep breath and tried to force herself to calm down.

Syrus turned her around and kissed her on the lips. "Don't worry. It will be easy. Dad's used to this kind of thing. He'll carry it through."

"I'm just glad I don't have to say anything. The very idea of public speaking of this magnitude turns me into a ball of jitters."

He smiled into her eyes. Everyday eye contact still felt so new to her, and her heart trembled in response.

He caught her chin. "I love you. You just remember that when you're up there."

"I will," she breathed, feeling more centered.

Forest used her trusty End of the Bridge to take them to Fortress Castle. The second their feet landed in the main foyer, they were bombarded with people. Servants and officials alike scrambled about to get their tasks done before the ceremony began.

"Forest! Syrus!" Zeren charged up and caught them both in a tight hug.

They groaned and straightened their clothing once he released them. Zeren clapped Syrus on the shoulder and turned his full attention to Forest. "Are you ready for this?" he asked.

"Yes. Do I look all right?"

"Perfect."

"Dad, have you seen Ithiel this morning?" Syrus asked.

"Not in the last hour, but I know he's here somewhere."

"I better go find him." Syrus kissed Forest bracingly. "I'll see you out there."

She watched Syrus absorb into the crowd.

"Come on." Zeren took her by the hand and towed her through the movement, out into the main courtyard.

The newly structured stage loomed before her. Her pulse tripped as she looked out over the size of the gathering crowd. The streets of Paradigm surged with people moving upward toward the castle. In a few minutes, she would stand shoulder to shoulder with Zeren, her father, and the rest of the *Rune-dy*, and the remaining members of Fortress' high council. The people would finally learn about the new structure of their world and see their combined leaders. There would be trouble and disagreements, skirmishes and dissention, but as Forest looked to the future, she saw only hope.

The gathering crowd packed in, every race mixing and standing together. She raised her head and looked out at them, unafraid and unashamed.

Epilogue

Forest rose with the sunrise. Syrus was already up and had her breakfast waiting. Their mornings weren't filled with chatter. They both readied for their days of work, touching each other whenever they passed.

So little time had passed in this newness of life, but Forest knew it would hold. Syrus would be with her for the rest of her life, and that alone was all she needed to be happy. They headed out of the house at the same time, Syrus locking the door behind him.

"Have you passed the legislation yet, lifting the ban on human goods?" he asked.

"It goes through next week. Why?"

"Well, Madam Hailemarris, you can't be a law breaker yourself. If anyone ever found out about the stuff in our house, it would cause a scandal."

Forest giggled. "Yeah. You're right. Do you have any new masters coming in today?"

"Tomorrow. Ithiel and I are prepping for them today."

He caught her chin in his hand at the gate and kissed her, looking deeply in her eyes with his new clear sight.

"Don't do that hypnotic stuff with those eyes when I'm leaving for work. It's not fair. Save it for the bedroom tonight."

He chuckled and kissed her again. "Just making sure you haven't grown immune to me."

She caught his bottom lip between her teeth and bit down. He groaned and crushed her against him. "Now you're not playing fair," he accused.

"Just making sure you haven't grown immune to me." She threw his words back at him with a saucy smile.

They passed through the gate and walked off in different directions. "I'll be home in time for S'mores," he called over his shoulder.

"Love you."

"Love you back."

The End

Acknowledgments

I'd like to give a big thank you to those who helped me write this book. First, to my dear friend, Amanda. I don't know how I'd break through writer's block without you. Second, a big shout out to my writers group. Each and every one of you has become a good friend. A special thanks to my angel editor, Claire Ashgrove. And to my husband, you are my real life alpha-male. Thank you for always letting me just be me.
 And lastly, a **huge** thank you to you, my reader!

For more information about Tenaya Jayne's books, visit her website at www.tenayajayne.com